The Ranger Boys and the Border Smugglers

Claude A. Labelle

THE RANGER BOYS AND THE BORDER SMUGGLERS

CHAPTER I.

OFF FOR NEW FIELDS.

"Now I believe you boys understand just what is wanted of you, as I explained it yesterday afternoon, but just to make sure, I'll go over it briefly again while you are waiting for your train," said the Customs Chief to the three Ranger Boys.

Our three friends were sitting in the office of the chief at the capitol in Maine, preparatory to bidding him goodbye before starting out for the Canadian border to try and run down a band of fur smugglers.

As they sit there, let us describe them and introduce them to those of our readers who have not read "The Ranger Boys to the Rescue," and "The Ranger Boys Find the Hermit."

First is Garfield Boone, known to his chums as Garry. He is the accepted and chosen leader of the trio on all their expeditions. Garry's father, known to the backwoodsmen as "Moose" Boone, is a wealthy lumberman.

Next is Phil Durant, a dark-haired youth of French descent. He is able to talk French fluently, but keeps this knowledge under cover, as the boys once found it useful for him to do. He is the son of a father and mother who are situated in very moderate circumstances.

Last, but by no means least, is Dick Wallace, the ward of Garry's father. Dick is the son of a college professor, who was a chum of Mr. Boone. He fell from a horse and injured his head when Dick was a youngster, and then disappeared. Dick's mother had died when he was a baby, so Mr. Boone took him into his own home to bring up. Dick, by the way, is rather fat; "plump" he calls himself.

These three boys form an extraordinary unit of the Maine Ranger service, that body of men whose duty it is to protect the great forest lands of the state from the danger of fire.

These boys were made Rangers through the influence of Mr. Boone, and had been in the woods about a month, where they had some stirring adventures, meeting an old hermit who has helped them, and making enemies of a half-breed guide, Jean LeBlanc, and a rascally ex-deputy Ranger, Anderson by name, who was supplanted by Nate Webster, a warm-hearted old Maine guide and a firm friend of the boys.

Among their adventures was the rescue of little Patty Graham, child of a rich broker who was camping in the woods, from the half-breed LeBlanc. As a reward for their brave deed, Mr. Graham presented them with a specially made wireless telephone outfit, complete with home station and compact carrying 'phones.

Now that we know who our heroes are, let us hear what the Customs Chief has to tell them.

"As I told you boys yesterday, this is our problem. We know that somewhere along the border, there is a regular smugglers' lane, where valuable shipments of seal and other furs have been smuggled into the United States with consequently a great loss of duty to the customs house. Now it is impossible for our men to find anything out, and if I get men from Washington, they don't know anything about the woods, so there you are.

"Now I think you boys can go up there, and by acting as campers, or even in your role of Rangers, you may find out just the things my agents have been unable to unearth. Ordinarily I wouldn't think of sending boys on this job, but you three have proven yourselves to be unusually alert andreliable, also being boys, you may not be regarded as dangerous by the woods people in that section.

"You had better go back to Bangor and have a conference with this man Webster, and get what supplies you need, then strike off across the state till you come to the border town of Hobart. That, I have reason to believe, is the base of operations of the smugglers.

"That I think is all. Before you go out, you will each be given a little gold customs badge. Secrete this somewhere on your persons and never show it

3

except as an absolute last resort. Also, you will be given one or two signals by means of which you may find out whether anyone is in the service or not. Now good luck go with you."

The Chief shook hands with the three, and they filed into the outer office where an assistant gave them their badges and some simple signals.

"If you should meet a man who gave his collar a tug at the throat as though it were too tight, you would think nothing of it, but if he gave it two little tugs, and then waited while you could count five and gave it three more little tugs, you would be told he was a customs man. Your reply would be two tugs, and in order to check up, he would give two more in answer. That is for meeting in a room, on a train, or in the street. If you should happen to be in a restaurant, the signal would be two taps of a cup on a saucer followed by three, or if it is a mug, the same number of taps against the table. Your answering signal would be the same. Don't ever do this just because you are inquisitive about a person. Have some sure grounds for believing that the man you are signalling is part of the service. Now goodbye and good fortune."

The boys left the capitol and made their way down the long hill to the main business part of the town.

As they struck onto the main business street, Garry noticed the familiar blue bell sign of the telephone company.

"Say, boys, I have an idea. Let's stop in here and put in long distance calls and say hello to our folks. How does the idea strike you?" said Garry, almost in one breath.

"Ripping," shouted Phil, while Dick didn't wait to make any remark, but dived in through the door, and in a trice was putting in his call. Phil followed suit, while Garry waited, as he would talk when Dick had finished.

This pleasant duty done, they went to a restaurant for dinner. Here they attracted no little attention, for their khaki clothes looked almost like uniforms. Added to this was the fact that they wore forest shoepacks, those high laced moccasins with an extra leather sole, and felt campaign hats.

Most of those who saw them, however, after an interested look, put them down as boys about to go on a camping trip, never dreaming that this same trio had been through more adventures in the previous month or so, than the average boy, or men, for that matter, has in half a dozen years.

Even the boys, hopeful as they were of adventures, did not dream of the stirring times that lay ahead of them in their quest of the border band of smugglers.

The boys thoroughly enjoyed the well-cooked, well-served meal, it being a welcome change to have someone else do their cooking for them.

"Eat up, fellows," advised Dick, who was ever ready to eat, "just two or three more restaurant meals, and then we'll be cooking our own again over a bed of red embers under the merry greenwood tree."

Luncheon over, the boys consulted a time-table and found they could get a train immediately or one quite late in the afternoon for Bangor.

"What say we take the late one, and go to a movie this afternoon?" queried Dick.

The matter was put up to Garry for a decision and as he was the leader his word always went, though he was never arbitrary and generally talked things over before making a real decision.

"I think we ought to take the early train. By doing that, we will get to Bangor at five o'clock, just the time we would be leaving here, should we take the later train. Then we can have dinner, see an early movie, and buy what few things we need and get a good sleep, for we have a two-day train journey. Doesn't that strike you fellows as the most logical thing to do?" he concluded.

Put to them in this light it seemed best, so it was unanimously agreed to start at once. They proceeded to the station where they had checked their rifles and knapsacks on leaving the hotel that morning.

"I must get several things when we get to Bangor," remarked Phil. "You know LeBlanc and Anderson stripped me of rifle, knife and axe that time they left me tied to the tree."

"Yes, you'll have to, also I am going to get a compass, as I lost mine the time I lost my way in the forest," said Garry.

"Well, all I've to get when we reach that city," announced Dick, "is something to eat!"

The others laughed and poked fun at Dick for his appetite, for his willingness to eat at any time of the day or night was a source of constant merriment to the other chums.

"Some day you will have to go a whole day without food, Dick," remarked Garry, "and I don't know what will happen to you. I imagine that you'll just wither up and die before help reaches you."

"Don't worry, I'll find some way to prevent going a day without a meal," said Dick emphatically.

The ride to Bangor was uneventful. As they passed through Waterville, they saw the great shaded campus of Colby College, deserted for the summer except for a few students who were pursuing extra courses.

"By golly, there's a pretty college there. I almost think I'd like to go there," remarked Dick.

"Well, according to things as they now stand, we have a couple of years to think that over," said Garry.

They reached the city of Bangor, on the wide Penobscot River about five o'clock. This city is famous for its paper mills and as a center for the gathering of lumberjacks for the woods work. Bangor is also famous for its great "Salmon Pool."

Garry remarked about this:

"Some first of April we must make plans to come up and try our luck at salmon."

"Why April first?" queried Phil.

"You see the law goes off at that time, and they are the best at that season. A little while later, during the spawning season, they are again protected. It is a wonderful sight, by the way, to see the twenty or twenty-five pound salmon jump up over falls and dams eight and ten feet in height. The Orono Indians, who used to inhabit this region, used to stand at the top of the falls and dexterously spear the fish as they jumped."

Supper was eaten at the Penobscot Exchange, and then the boys journeyed down Canal Street to an old store where they intended to get a new rifle and some other things. They found the old gunsmith was out and would not be back until about eleven o'clock, so decided to go to the movies, and return at that hour.

They enjoyed the motion picture show immensely, particularly because one of the scenes in the News Weekly showed forest fire fighters combatting the flames in the Michigan woods.

After the show they made their way back towards the old gunsmith's shop. The street was deserted save for a party of roisterers, who passed them, singing at the top of their voices. They were passing a badly lighted spot, when, from a ramshackle old three-story house, they heard a shriek followed by an appeal for mercy.

CHAPTER II.

THE OLD HOUSE.

"Did you hear a scream, Garry?" asked Dick, as he stopped in his tracks.

"I am sure I did, Dick," answered the leader, "but I was wondering whether it meant anything. You know this isn't the quietest and most lamb-like part of the city, it is probably only some carousing lumberjacks."

"Let's wait a minute or two and see if we can hear anything more," suggested Phil.

They waited a short time, and were about to move on, when the scream was repeated, and the boys distinctly heard a call for help.

"All set, boys, let's see what this is all about," cried Dick, who though fat, and sometimes inclined to take things easily, was not a bit of a coward.

"Wait a minute, fellows, let's see what our plan is," said Garry, hurriedly. "Remember we have no weapons, so every move must be made carefully. There are three floors. Dick, take the top, Phil you search the second, I'll take the ground floor. Go through the halls, listen carefully, and at the first sign of anything, whistle three times and the others will join whoever gives the whistle. Now, let's go!"

"One more thing," said Garry; "when you climb the stairs, step on the end either near the wall or the balustrade, then the steps won't be so apt to creak."

They found the front door open and made their way inside. The interior of the house was in inky blackness.

"Careful, now," warned Garry. "Whistle at the first sign of trouble, no matter how slight it is."

Phil and Dick sprang up the stairs, noiselessly, yet speedily. There was not a sign of noise, all was as quiet as a cemetery at midnight.

Left alone, Garry went along the hall, stopping at each door and listening intently. He was unrewarded until he came to the end door.

Here he thought he heard a sound of scuffling and squealing. Cautiously he tried the door, holding a flashlight ready in his hand. As he opened the door and stepped into the darkness, he saw the gleam of two small eyes, then heard a frightened scampering across the floor.

Garry snapped on his flashlight and then gave a relieved laugh. The noise had been caused by nothing more than a pair of rats, who had been feasting on the remains of a supper on a rickety old table.

The broken bits of food, the unwashed dishes, and the empty cans showed that someone evidently lived in the house, and only recently and probably surreptitiously as the thick dust that lay everywhere seemed to indicate that the house had not been regularly occupied for some time.

Garry saw a door at one side of the kitchen, for that was the room into which he had penetrated, and carefully opened it. The door led into a long room, with a half a dozen tables, bare of cloth, and with chairs stacked on them.

From the appearance of this room, and judging by the big range in the kitchen from which he had just come, Garry decided that the house was used in the winter as a boarding house for lumberjacks.

He went back to the kitchen and opened the only other door. A cool draft told him this was the cellar, and he listened intently, then flashing his light, went down the steps. A few moments' investigation showed him that there was no living person down there. The air was musty, and the cellar seemed damp.

While Garry was examining the lower floor, Phil and Dick had gone up the stairs. Here, too, all was quiet. Wishing Phil a hasty good luck, Dick began the ascent of the flight that led to the third floor.

Left alone, Phil stood stockstill for a few minutes, getting his bearings. There was a long hall from which led off ten doors, five on either side.

Phil decided he could do nothing better than go from door to door, listening intently at each one, then enter the room and flash his light about, for each of the boys had provided himself with a heavy battered flashlamp.

He wondered where the screams could have come from, as there wasn't a sound of anyone stirring on the floor. He could hear Dick's stealthy footfall above him occasionally.

He listened at each door intently, and peered at them for a sign of light creeping through a keyhole or chance crack, but his vigilance went unrewarded.

Finally at the very last door he saw a mere speck of light through the keyhole. He dropped to his knee and glued his eye to the keyhole. By the flaring light of a couple of candles stuck into bottles, he could make out the still form of a man on a cot.

The room was considerably torn up, as though a search for something had been made.

Then a man crossed his line of vision and shook up the form on the cot. The sleeping, or unconscious man, made no move, and the other disappeared for a moment and then returned, bearing a small pail containing water which he proceeded to splash vigorously on the face of the recumbent man.

Presently this had its desired effect for the form stirred, and in a voice hardly above a whisper the man began to speak.

Phil could not distinguish the words, but the other spoke loudly, and Phil heard him say:

"Now listen here. You come through with that map, or I'll leave you here to be carried out feet first!"

The old man feebly protested and Phil was about to whistle for help when he saw the assailant rip away the old man's shirt and disclose a cloth bag. It was the work of a second to tear this open and extract from it a paper.

Phil could hear the chuckle of satisfaction and then he gasped, for the old man rose from his cot and tried to grapple with the younger man, who gave him a brutal push, throwing him back onto the cot.

Phil hesitated no longer, and so excited was he that he failed to give the signal. Throwing open the door, he rushed into the room, and directing the flashlight directly into the eyes of the man, partially blinded him. At the same moment he made a grab for the paper, but succeeded only in getting a part of it, one piece remaining in the hands of the man.

The old man lay back on the cot gasping for breath, so could be of no harm, nor yet of any assistance. The younger man was undersized, hardlymore than a match for Phil, who was an exceptionally strong lad, yet so great was the evident worth of the paper, that he started for Phil, slowly and warily.

Phil was unarmed, but a happy stratagem occurred to him. Hastily reaching into his pocket, he drew forth a shiny pair of wire cutters, and pointed them at the culprit, at the same time ordering him to throw up his hands.

The momentary gleam of the polished wire cutters was enough to convince the man that a pistol was being pointed at him, but instead of obeying the order to hoist his hands, he made a spring for an open window, jumped over the sill, and a bare second later, Phil heard a dull thud.

He dashed to the window and flashed his light about, to find that a very few feet below was an ell roof, and he just caught a glimpse of the fugitive letting himself over the edge, probably to drop into a yard below and so make his way to freedom.

Foiled in his attempt to capture the fellow, Phil turned his attention to the old man. He shoved the paper, the seeming cause of all the trouble, into his hands and told him he had nothing more to worry about.

To his surprise, however, the old man weakly pushed it back to him, saying in laborious gasps:

"Take it, boy, it's yours. I'm — going — out — a fortune in — — "

His words trailed into nothingness and he dropped back, ceasing to breathe. Startled, and a little bit frightened, Phil ran and put a hand to his heart. There was no vibrating response.

Stuffing the paper into his jacket pocket, he ran to the door and gave two low but distinct whistles. Hardly had he given the signal when there was an unearthly crash and a muttered expression of disgust.

Phil made for the stairs, and was about to descend when he was joined by Dick, who whispered sibilantly:

"Dig out of here; this is no place for us," and seizing Phil by the arm, started down the stairway. At the bottom they found Garry extricating himself from a heap of splintered wood and debris.

"All out in a hurry," commanded Dick.

Garry and Phil both sensed that there was danger in the air, or, at the very least, a need for extra care, and followed the lead of Dick in making a quick exit from the house.

They hustled down the sidewalk, and noticing an open hallway, unlighted, Dick led the way in there.

"Not a whisper, now," he cautioned.

Hardly had they found shelter in the doorway when three men came tumbling out of the deserted lodging house they had just left, and ran past the hallway where the boys were crouching, finally to disappear around a corner farther up the street.

"Say, for the love of Pete, Dick, what's all this mystery about, and who found anything and where did the screams come from?" queried Garry, amazed at the strange turn events had taken.

Dick was about to make a reply, when Phil interrupted.

"All our stories can wait. First we must get the police. I've just left a dead man, and I have good reason to believe there was foul play."

"Then let's save our breath and hustle after an officer; we can compare notes later," said Garry.

They branched off Canal Street, up through a narrow thoroughfare, more alley than street, and soon found themselves on a well lighted business street. Here they moderated their pace, and after a brisk walk of three blocks, saw a policeman.

"You're the spokesman in this case, Phil, you know what this is all about, and we don't," directed Garry.

Approaching the officer, Phil stated the case. The policeman looked at them curiously, then appeared to be convinced of their honesty, and turning to a police box, notified the station, asking that the night lieutenant come at once. He told his superior where the place was, for knowing that section of the city, thoroughly, he immediately recognized it from Phil's description.

They made their way back, and going up the stairs, went at once to the room. Here the police officer looked about and then asked a few perfunctory questions of the boys.

"I guess you fellows better wait here till the lieutenant comes," he said finally.

"Does that mean we are under arrest?" queried Garry.

"No indeed, just a formality. You see that is what I have to do in all cases like this, but you can tell your story to the lieutenant."

They waited a few minutes and then the sound of tramping feet was heard on the stairs and the lieutenant of the police force entered the room followed by a man carrying a black bag, evidently a doctor and probably the coroner.

The police officer cast a scrutinizing look over the room and then waved the doctor to make his examination. This took only a few minutes.

"What do you find Doc?" asked the officer familiarly.

"This man was stabbed or cut some time ago, probably two or three weeks, but the cause of his death seems to be heart failure, induced no doubt by lack of care, improper nourishment, and a severe shock that finished him off with his organically weak heart."

"What do you mean, stabbed or cut, accidentally?" asked the officer gruffly.

"Not accidentally, but by a blow inflicted by someone," returned the doctor.

"What do you chaps know about this?" he asked, turning suddenly on the three boys. Garry opened his mouth to answer.

"We——"

"Wait till I get through talking before you are spoken to. What are you chaps, runaways, and where did you get those clothes, steal 'em?"

A dark flush crept up under Garry's ears.

"Look here officer, you keep a civil tongue in your head, with all due respect to your rank and authority, and before we answer any questions, just what is our status now?" he said.

"If you mean, are you under arrest, you are!"

CHAPTER III.

IN THE HANDS OF THE LAW.

Arrested!

Both Dick and Phil started to make a vociferous protest but were quickly silenced by Garry.

"All right, officer. But we answer no more of your questions and ask to be taken immediately to the station and the services of a lawyer procured for us," said Garry firmly.

"Huh, pretty smart youngsters, aren't you. Well, let me tell you one thing, laddy buck. You'll answer any questions I ask of you and answer them quick. Now who are you and how were you in this room at the time this man died — or was killed," said the officer in a threatening tone.

The three boys held their silence, taking their cue from their leader, Garry.

"Won't talk, eh, well we'll make you open your mouth in a hurry," and the officer advanced on the boys.

Just what steps he would have taken will never be known, for the physician, who was the city coroner, interposed.

"That will do, Murphy. You have just told these boys they were under arrest, and you have failed to give them warning that anything they may say can be used against them. You are barking up the wrong tree anyway. These are no runaways nor young desperadoes. My advice is that you let them go immediately, or else take them to the station and let the chief talk to them. He was still there when we left the house. And, boys, I'll see that you get a lawyer as soon as you get there unless the captain shows more sense than the lieutenant has."

The lieutenant glowered at the coroner. Evidently there was bad blood between them, but he realized that he had overstepped his authority, and was in the wrong, so he ordered everyone present to repair to the station.

The walk to the headquarters of the city police consumed only a few minutes, and soon the boys were standing in the office of the Chief.

"What's all this, Lieutenant Murphy?" he asked.

"There's been foul play of some sort down in that old shack that's used in the wintertime for a lumberjack boarding house. These three boys were there at the time the man died and don't seem to be able to give a satisfactory account of themselves. They have been put under arrest," answered the officer sulkily.

"Well, boys, what have you to say to this," asked the Chief as he swung around on his chair and surveyed the three.

By this time Garry was boiling mad.

"I first want to ask that we get a lawyer. I don't propose to have a continuation of the bullying that the lieutenant started down at the old shack continued, nor do I propose to let my companions be questioned without competent advice," he said respectfully but decidedly.

The Chief's face darkened.

"Have you been up to your old tricks again, Murphy?"

"I've just been doing my duty," said Murphy sullenly.

"I am afraid you exaggerate your duty at times, then, lieutenant. Now, boys, what have you to say? This is only an informal questioning and you are under no obligations to answer. I think, however, that there has been nothing more here than the stirring up of a mare's nest, and I think the best thing to do is to come out and say what you have to say. If there is nothing against you, then that is your best course."

Garry recognized that the Chief was a fair man, and decided to tell their story.

"We are Forest Rangers, sir, just going to a new post of duty. We were down on that street in search of a gunsmith's shop to procure a new rifle to replace one that one of my companions lost. We heard screams coming from the old house and ran to see if we could be of assistance. One of the boys found the old man who is now dead being attacked by a younger man. He was driven out, making his escape by a window and over the roof of the ell. Then we went and summoned the policeman from his beat, and now here we are."

"How does it happen you do all the talking?" asked the Chief.

"Why, the boys have seen fit to make me the leader and spokesman at all times. We have always done that."

"You seem to tell a straight enough story in some ways," said the Chief. "But I have seen a good many Forest Ranger service men go through this town, and I never saw boys doing that work before. As far as the death of the old man is concerned, I see nothing to hold you on, as I understand that he died and was not killed while you were there. I am inclined to think you are stretching things a bit, however, when you claim to be Rangers. You are sure you boys aren't making tracks for the Big Woods in search of supposed adventure, are you?"

"That is the second time tonight that we have been accused of that, and it is getting a bit tiresome. I think we can satisfy you very quickly, however. There are probably men in town who know my father, who is part owner of the pulp mills up the river. The best way, however, is to get the Chief Ranger, Mr. Ardmore, on the long distance 'phone. Till then I think we won't say anything more."

The Chief looked at them quizically for a moment. He was still inclined to be suspicious, but the mention of Garry's father made him think that perhaps he was on the wrong track. He pulled an extension 'phone to him, and called the long distance operator.

"This is the Chief of Police talking," he said. "I want you to get the Chief Forest Ranger, Mr. Ardmore, at Augusta. You can get his home telephone number from the night operator at the State House. This is an emergency, so rush it through," and he replaced the receiver on the hook.

"That will do for now, Murphy, and Coroner, I suppose you want to make out your report. You will find a desk not in use in the next room. In the meantime, you boys make yourselves comfortable for a few minutes, I don't expect that the call will be more than five minutes in going through," and the Chief began to busy himself with some papers around his desk.

The boys withdrew to a corner of the room, and found chairs.

The minutes seemed to drag horribly. None of the boys was exactly worried, except for the fact that they were losing precious time. They wanted to go back to Canal Street and buy the rifle and such other things as they might need. If they were held for some sort of a hearing in the morning, it would delay them considerably as their train left early, and there was no other until late in the afternoon, meaning they would lose almost a day on their journey.

After a few minutes of silence, Dick cautiously whispered to Garry, "How about showing him our customs papers and badges?"

"Only as a last resort," answered Garry in a low tone.

They looked up when they saw the Chief reaching for the telephone.

"How about that Augusta call?"

He listened a moment, then hung up the receiver and turned to the boys.

"Operator says she is still working on it, that they cannot find him now, but are trying places where he might be. Still of the opinion you want me to talk to him?"

"Positively," answered Garry.

The Chief resumed his newspaper, and the boys fidgeted a minute until Garry bethought himself of the pocket checkerboard they generally carried. He fished it out and suggested they play to while away the time. Dick elected to play first with Garry, and let Phil take on the winner.

Seeing them at their game, the Chief walked over and stood watching. Garry had just succeeded in getting a king after an unusually clever play, and the Chief, who was quite a player himself, was applauding softly when the 'phone bell rang.

"Guess there's our call now," he remarked, as he hurried back to his desk.

Sure enough it was the call, and in a moment the Chief was talking with Mr. Ardmore.

"Listen, Mr. Ardmore, this is the Chief of Police of Bangor. I have three boys here who were picked up after finding a dead man in a room here. There is nothing against them on that score, but they claim to be Forest Rangers, and I say they are too young, so to settle the matter I am calling you. They give their names as Boone, Wallace and Durant," and here the Chief described them. "They're all right, you say?" queried the Chief, in a slightly surprised tone. "All right, guess I was wrong then. All right, here's one right here." Then he turned to Garry and said:

"He wants to talk to you."

Garry exchanged greetings with the Chief Ranger and heard him say:

"Can't you three take a step without running smack into something exciting? I declare, you fellows see more and do more than men who have ranged the woods for these past ten years. Keep it up, and keep out of trouble. Write me all about this, not an official report, only a personal letter, to satisfy my own curiosity. Best of luck to the others. Goodbye. I had to leave the theatre to answer this call, and I am anxious to get back to my seat."

Garry hung up the receiver, and then turned and asked the Chief if he was satisfied.

"Indeed I am, and I wish you boys all the luck in the world in your new station," said the Chief. The three boys then took their leave. They returned immediately to Canal Street to see if they were still in time to buy a rifle for Phil from the old gunsmith.

They arrived at the shop just in time to find him locking the door. He recognized them immediately, and had no hesitancy in opening up his store again. Phil soon found a rifle to his liking, and Garry replaced the compass that he had dropped when he was lost in the woods; ammunition was also procured, and then Garry purchased a small automatic revolver, deciding that this would be a wise project in view of the kind of work that they might be called upon to do in running down the band of smugglers.

"Now," said Garry, "I wonder if there is anything more that we will need?"

"Yes," said Dick, "I think we should procure new, heavy pocket knives. I have broken the big blade of mine, and you remember that Phil's was taken away from him by LeBlanc and Anderson that time that they left him tied to the tree in the forest."

"That is a wise suggestion," remarked Garry, as he turned to the old man and asked to see something in combination knives.

"Here is something that I frequently sell, both to campers and woodsmen," said the old gunsmith. "You see it has one heavy blade, suitable for skinning a small animal, and in addition has a heavy canopener."

The knives met all requirements, so each boy procured one. The last thing bought was an ample supply of batteries for their flashlights.

"There," said Garry, "I think that completes everything we have to buy except a supply of food. We can get that in the morning, and I have some ideas of what we should buy. Of course, this time we won't have to supply ourselves with enough food for a month, as we will probably make the town of Hobart our base of supplies. However, my idea is to get a very small compact bundle of concentrated foods, such as bar chocolate and highly concentrated soup. This, with a small portion of tea and coffee, can be packed into a very small bundle, and yet were one lost in the woods, he would find that such a supply would last him more than a week."

Bidding the old gunsmith goodnight, they returned to the hotel, meeting Lieut. Murphy on the way. "Sure boys, I hope you will forget everything that has happened this evening. It was only last week that I picked up three boys who were going up into the woods to shoot Indians, and I didn't know but that you might be tarred with the same brush."

"Don't let that bother you at all, Lieutenant. I suppose you have to do your duty just as you see it, so we will forget about it, and say goodnight."

They reached the Penobscot Exchange, and getting their key from the clerk, went directly to their room. As Garry popped open the door, he uttered a shout of surprise, for there, making himself comfortable in an easy chair, sat Nate Webster.

CHAPTER IV.

THE TORN MAP.

"Well," said Nate, "it seems to me you fellows keep rather late hours. I have been waiting for you upwards of two hours. Where have you been keeping yourself? I calculate likely as not you fellows have been to a theatre."

"Half of your guess is correct," said Garry, with a laugh, "but since leaving the show, we have had a wild time. First place, we found a dead man, and second place, we got arrested."

"'Sho' now, you don't say so. What have you fellows been doing that got you in the grip of the law?"

"Why, as to that, Nate, I can hardly say myself," said Garry. "Things came so thick and fast, that I haven't yet found out what it was all about, so I think now would be as good a time as any for each one of us to tell his story, and just for the sake of having things in order, and because I have so little to tell, I will take the first turn. When we went into the old abandoned boarding house, for such as I discovered it to be, I searched the entire lower floor and the cellar, and finding nothing, was about to make my way up the stairs, when I leaned too heavy against the balustrade, and in another moment I found myself crashing to the floor below. Next thing I knew, Dick and Phil here came tumbling out after me, and in another few moments, we found ourselves arrested and taken to the police station; now that lets me out. Now Dick, your story is the next shortest, and I don't suppose that anything happened to you that was any more exciting than my search."

"Don't you fool yourself on that score," said Dick, "because I think I have some very startling news. There has been so much excitement in the last hour or two that I have given little or no thought to it. I went, as you know, to the top floor, and there hearing nothing or seeing no light, I simply crept from door to door, peeking through the keyhole, and then listening closely to see if I could hear anything stirring within. Search of several doors revealed nothing, until I came to one back of which I believed was several men, as I seemed to hear a low murmur of voices. The keyhole was plugged up, so I got down on my knees; I could see no light coming out from beneath the door. I was certain someone was in the room, so very cautiously I turned the handle, but the door refused to budge an inch. However, there was one way to find out. In getting out my knife, I drilled a small hole through the door, using the point of the knife. I had no sooner finished this, when a small gleam of light came through the door, showing that I had not been wrong in my conclusions. Without making any noise, I enlarged the hole, so that I could get a clearer view of the room. There were three men sitting about a table, playing cards. It was certain that the screams did not come from this room, and I was about to knock on the door, when suddenly I recognized the men. You remember the week before we went into the big woods, and the adventure we had when we caught the three tramps in our shack by the river? Well, right there, sitting at that table, were the identical three men for whom we received the reward!"

"You must be mistaken Dick," remarked Garry. "Those three were dangerous men, but I don't believe they could have escaped from the jail in Portland."

"Nevertheless," said Dick, "I am absolutely certain that those are the three. There are any number of ways in which they might have gotten away. There is even a chance that they have been tried by this time, and have been released."

"That seems hardly possible," interrupted Phil. "The authorities were sure they had the right men or they would never have given us the reward."

The entire matter was very puzzling to the boys, when Nate, who was always on the job, broke in with a suggestion. "Why don't you fellows telephone down to 'Moose Boone' and ask him if the tramps got away."

"I don't think he would know anything about it," said Garry, "for I was talking with him on the 'phone, when we were in Augusta, and he didn't make any mention of it."

Then Dick came to bat with a suggestion. "Why don't we telephone to Sam Preston, the newspaper man, surely he would know if anybody would." The call was immediately put in, and while they were waiting for an answer, they made use of the opportunity, and asked Nate how it was he happened to be there. "Why, I simply got a long distance call from the Chief Ranger, asking me to meet you boys here, to give you whatever suggestions I could as to the place you are going, and also to see if I could remember the names of two or three of my friends in that part of the country who might be of some help when you need it."

"Why, of course, Garry," remarked Dick, "you remember the Chief of Customs telling us he would arrange to have Nate meet us here? However, perhaps we had better defer getting any advice from Nate until Phil has told his story."

That moment the telephone rang, and on answering it, Garry found that the person on the other end of the wire was Sam Preston. After chatting a moment with Sam, he asked if there was any news of the three burglars whom they had caught early in the summer. There was silence for several moments in the room, while Sam talked, and then with a goodbye, Garry replaced the receiver on the hook, and turned around to face his companions.

"Well, Dick, you sure hit the matter about right. The three burglars were brought up for a hearing, and were allowed to go free on bail, pending their trial. They took advantage of the opportunity to disappear. Now the authorities of Portland are searching high and low for them."

"Yes," said Dick, "the reason I hurried out of the house there, bringing you fellows with me, was because I saw one of them starting toward the door, and believe me, I knew more than to stack up against three of them all alone. We have made enough enemies in the past few weeks without getting others on our trail.

"That is something we can discuss later. I suggest now that Phil tell us what happened on the second floor, as he seems to be the one that had the real adventure of the night." Phil told his story, and in the speaking of it, recollected the torn piece of paper that the old man with his dying words had given him. He pulled it from his pocket, and the three boys, as well as Nate, spread it out on the table and began to examine it. It seemed to be a rough, crudely drawn map with a dotted line, running from the spot marked by a figure 1, with a circle drawn around it. The dotted line, however, unfortunately ran direct to the part that had been torn off when Phil seized the paper from the old man's assailant. On the reverse of the paper, written in a laborious and cramped hand, was the following inscription: "The lost mine lies 100 paces from the spot marked 2. The land mark noted on the map as figure 1, is a ravine, exactly two miles east of the Shohela River, at the point where it makes a sharp turn above the town of Jennings. Start at the mouth of that ravine and travel directly north for about two miles and one-half, until you come to − − "

Here the boys found that the missing part of the note corresponded to the portion which had been torn off during the struggle.

"Well," said Nate, "the pesky map doesn't mean to do you much good now, does it? I know of the place mentioned in that note, but I have never been there, so I can't tell you much about what the old something or other might be. Without wanting to throw any cold water upon your plans, I should say to forget about the whole business. I know the Maine woods pretty well, and I never heard tell of any mines which have been found in this part of the country, except, maybe, limestone mines, and surely nobody would have a secret map as to where a limestone mine would be, so I think you had better just tuck that piece of paper away and forget all about it."

The boys, however, with romantic ideas of finding a lost gold mine hidden away somewhere in the wilds of the Maine woods, refused to be discouraged by Nate's pessimistic remarks, and each one decided, that at the first opportunity, they would visit the scene told of in the map, and see if possible they could not discover the secret of the lost mine.

"Now boys," said Nate, "we might as well get over the main business of the evening, that being to tell you about what I know about Hobart. It has been a good many years since I was in that part of the woods, but I remember it as well as though I had been there only yesterday. Hobart is a small town, nowhere near the size of Millinocket. About ten years ago it was the center of industrial lumbering operations. As a matter of fact, Garry, I believe that your father was interested in the timber cutting of that place at that time. It is only four or five miles away from the Canadian border, and about fifty miles to the south the States of Maine and New Hampshire and the Dominion of Canada are joined together. It is right about that point, also, that is, where the three territories come together, that the National Forest Preserve begins; that you know, without my telling you, is the movement recently started by the Government for conservation of the timber lands of the State. Eventually, every bit of forest land in the State will be under the control of the government. That means that timber cruisers, appointed by the government, will go on everybody's land, marking the trees that may properly be cut. This will prevent ruthless timber owners from clean cutting great tracts of land, and there will be a perpetual source of new timber."

"As for the town of Hobart itself, I have been trying to think ever since I heard from Augusta of some people that I knew there, but can't seem to remember a single one. However, as soon as I get back home, I will inquire from Silas Peabody and some of the other guides if they remember any people in that section, and I can write you in care of the postmaster at Hobart. However, I will warn you of this, that as I remember it, it was a mighty tough town, — border towns nearly always are, — for you get a good deal of the rougher element of both countries. That doesn't mean, ofcourse, that you won't find a few mighty nice people up there, although I don't suppose your work will allow you to make many friends. I am sorry that I can't tell you more about the country, but I don't doubt that you will be able to take care of yourselves as well there as you have in your first station. The only thing I do hope is that you have seen the end of LeBlanc and his friend."

The hour by this time had grown late, so the boys all hopped into bed. Nate retired to his own room, promising to arouse them at an early hour, so that they might get a good start for their new station.

CHAPTER V.

PHIL GETS A CLUE.

True to his word, old Nate woke the boys up almost with the dawn. Hurrying into their clothes, they went into the dining-room, where a sleepy waitress took their orders for a substantial breakfast. They chatted merrily with Nate during the meal, and then bade him goodbye, as his train went an hour earlier than theirs. Nothing remained for them to do in Bangor except to buy the provisions that Garry had spoken of the previous night. They found what they sought at a large grocery store which, on account of the early hour, had barely opened its doors for business.

"There," said Garry, "that completes our work in Bangor. We might as well take a last look at the town, because it is probable that we won't come back here for some time."

They proceeded to the station and found that their train was being made up at that moment.

"I suggest that we take seats in the smoker," remarked Garry, "for although none of us smoke, we might make some acquaintance there as we did with Nate when we first went into the big woods."

This suggestion met with hearty approval from the boys, and being the first on the train, they were able to pick a double seat, and found plenty of room in which to stow away their knapsacks and rifles. The train slowly filled up with a motley assemblage. There were several men in the usual garb of the forests, as well as a number of farmers. Two or three well dressed men looked as though they might be traveling salesmen. Half a dozen card games were soon started, and the boys found plenty to watch and thus occupy their time. Directly in back of Phil sat two men clad in rough corduroys and high boots. Both of the men were talking confidentially in the French language. Phil, as our readers know, was as conversant with French as he was with English, and for a time paid no attention to the remarks of the pair in back of him. Garry and Dick, in the meantime, were chatting away like a couple of magpies.

Suddenly Phil pricked up his ears and after a moment signalled his two chums to keep silent.

Garry immediately had a hunch that Phil was hearing something that might prove to be of advantage to them later on, so in order that their silence might not be noticed, fished out the pocket checkerboard, and soon he and Dick were immersed in the intricacies of the game, leaving Phil free to devote his entire attention to the conversation that was taking place in back of him.

After nearly a half of an hour, Phil lifted his head, and catching the eye of Garry, made it known to him that he wanted him to follow him out. Getting up and stretching, Phil nonchalantly made his way into another car, followed shortly by both Garry and Dick. Finding seats in the far end of the car, where their conversation could not be overheard, Garry eagerly inquired what Phil had heard.

"I want both of you boys," remarked Phil, "to pay special attention to those two men who were sitting in back of me, and impress their appearance upon your memories, as I believe they are the first clue to our mission at Hobart. Unfortunately, they do not talk very much about their plans, but from what I gather, they are on their way there to purchase furs, and they made special remarks about the good bargains they could drive, hinting at the fact that the furs were smuggled in across the border. Of course, it is hardly probable that they belong to the smugglers' gang, although, if we keep close tabs on them, it seems to me that they will eventually lead us to the headquarters of the border smugglers."

"Don't you think you should have stayed there?" inquired Garry.

"No, it was safe enough to leave," answered Phil, "because they had begun to talk on entirely different topics, one remarking to the other that they had better stop further talk of the furs, for fear they might be overheard by someone. Fortunately for us, they have no idea that they have already been overheard."

"There is one thing we ought to consider," said Garry. "In the event that they get off the train before we do, it seems to me that one of us should get off at that same time and follow them. Whoever it is can leave his knapsack and rifle behind, and the remaining two will take care of them. In the event of such a thing, boys, I would recommend that Phil be the one to get off the train, as he is the only one of us whose knowledge of French is great enough to allow him to understand what a native Frenchman is saying."

This plan being decided upon, the boys made their way back to the smoker. The two men had left their seats, and for a moment the boys were worried, then remembered that no stop had been made during the time which they had left the smoking car. A hasty search soon revealed the fact that the men had joined in a card game at the far end of the car. Knowing that the men would not talk business while in the game, the boys did not bother to try and find some way of overhearing their conversation.

The boys, in guarded tones, so that they might not be overheard by anyone in an adjoining seat, talked over the importance of the clue, that they had so fortunately stumbled upon.

"It strikes me that this is our lucky morning," remarked Garry. "Here we might have been days and days before we ever found the slightest bit of evidence on which to base our search for the band of smugglers, but in less than an hour after the starting of our mission, we stumble upon this very important bit of help."

As Garry talked, he kept glancing out of the corner of his eye at a tall, rangy individual, who since the boys had entered the car, had kept constant watch on them.

"Don't look up now," he whispered to his companions, "but a few minutes later casually glance across the aisle two seats up from where we are sitting, and look at that tall chap who is sitting there reading a newspaper. Ever since we got on board the train he has been watching us over the top of the paper. I wonder if there isn't some way in which we could get into conversation with him, and see who he is."

The words were hardly out of Garry's mouth, and before his chums had had a chance to survey the stranger, the object of their conversation threw down his newspaper and getting up sauntered over to where the trio was sitting. The boys looked up and gazed inquiringly at the newcomer, who seemed not a whit abashed at their scrutiny.

"Going on a camping trip?" he inquired with a pleasant smile.

"Why yes, we are," said Garry quickly, before either of the others could make a reply. "Are you also?" for Garry had noticed that a cased rifle and blanket roll were stowed under the stranger's seat.

"Why yes and no," answered the stranger. "I am going partly on business and partly on pleasure. Mind if I sit in with you a few minutes"

"Why, no indeed," said Garry cordially, as he moved over and made room for the tall stranger. "I suppose we might as well make ourselves acquainted, so I will start in by introducing myself. My name is Garry Boone, and these are my two chums, Dick Wallace and Phil Durant."

"My name is Fernald, Arthur Fernald, having no particular home, nor any particular business. Where are you boys bound for?"

"Why," said Garry, after a moment's hesitation, "we're bound for the border, but just where we will make our headquarters we do not know as yet, probably just whatever the fancy seizes us."

"Expect to get any hunting?" inquired the stranger. "Some mighty fine specimens of moose and caribou are to be found in that locality."

This remark made Garry suspicious, and he immediately shot this question at the stranger. "Don't you know that the law is on moose and caribou, and that there won't be an open season for at least five more years?"

"Yes," said the stranger, laconically. "I just wanted to see whether you boys knew that."

Garry was inclined to be angry at the man's answer, but as Fernald made the remark with a smile, Garry felt that they could not take offence at him.

Dick broke into the conversation with a query as to whether the stranger knew anything about the town of Hobart. Too late, Garry gave him a warning kick, but the danger was done. Fernald looked intently at Dick, and then at the other two.

"Why, yes," he remarked, "I know considerable about the town. It is only two or three weeks since I have been there. Anything in particular that you want to know about it?"

"Not especially," answered Dick, who was on guard now that Garry had warned him. "We just happened to hear a friend of ours, a guide named Webster, saying that it was not very far above the National Forest Reserve."

"You aren't, by any chance, speaking of Nate Webster of Millinocket are you?" he inquired with a smile.

Here Garry broke in the conversation.

"Do you know Webster?"

"I should say I do," said Fernald. "I have known him for a good many years. It may surprise you to know and hear," he turned to Garry, "that I know your father, 'Moose' Boone."

This, for a moment, seemed to free the man of suspicion, although, as Garry told himself, the man had not said or done anything to warrant their being suspicious of him. Garry was simply following the wise rule not to tell any more about yourself than the other person does to you.

They chatted for some time about many things concerning the woods, and while the boys were careful not to mention anything that would give the man who called himself Fernald any inkling as to their mission, they could not help notice but that he was trying very hard to pump them as to their reason for going to the particular part of Maine for which they were bound. By this time, it was nearly noon and Fernald volunteered the information that there was a restaurant in the station of a little town where they would make their next stop, and at which the train would stop long enough to allow them to get their lunch. Just before the train drew into the station, Fernald remarked in a bantering tone, "I suppose you fellows know there is considerable smuggling going on all the time, across the International line."

Garry looked up quickly, and met the stranger's quizzical glance squarely. "Why, I suppose I have heard about as much of it as the average citizen of Maine has. Why do you ask that question? Do you know anything special about it?"

"No," answered the stranger, "I was just merely asking for the sake of asking a question. Well, so long boys, I may see you at luncheon, just now I want to finish an article I was reading in a newspaper about the low price that furs are bringing this summer."

With that as a parting shot, he returned to his seat, leaving the three boys wondering just who he might be.

"I am very suspicious about this man Fernald," Garry told his two companions. "He seems very anxious to know all about our business, and his two hints about smuggling and the low price of furs lead me to believe that he was trying to pump us. Do you fellows think the same, or am I unduly suspicious?"

Phil, who was naturally a solid-headed boy, thought for a moment, and then agreed that there was something mighty peculiar about the actions oftheir new acquaintance, while Dick claimed that he had been suspicious of him from the moment that he had first come over to their seat.

By this time the train drew into the station, and the boys hastened out of the train and into the restaurant, where they were soon eating a hearty meal. They were joined by Fernald, who took the vacant seat opposite Garry. Fernald ordered a cup of coffee to be brought to him immediately, and suddenly, to the amazement of the boys, he looked straight at Garry, and gave his cup two sharp raps against the edge of the saucer. He waited a moment, and followed this by three taps. Garry waited for an instant, and then deciding to find out whether or not the tapping was accidental, gave the same signal. The man called Fernald smiled, and gave two soft taps of the cup before he replaced it on the saucer. The man of whom they had been so suspicious during the last hour, was unmistakably a customs officer!

CHAPTER VI.

THE NEW STATION.

"Listen, boys, not a word. Wait till we get back on the train, where the rumbling of the wheels over the rails will help to cover our words. Even if we could talk without danger of being overheard, we would not have time, for this train stops barely long enough to allow one to eat."

The boys made haste to finish the meal. They had not recovered from their surprise at finding the stranger was a customs agent even by the time they were through eating and were back in their seats in the smoking car.

"I don't suppose you boys have even started to formulate a plan of campaign, have you?" asked Fernald.

"Not yet, sir," replied Garry. "That is, we haven't made up our minds how to proceed after we have arrived at our headquarters. However, we have stumbled, or rather Phil has, on what we consider to be a very important clue, if such it may be called."

Garry's eyes swept the car, and in a moment he had located the two fur dealers, who had spoken of the cheap furs to be bought near the border.

"Do you see the two men who are in the fourth seat from the front of the car, facing us and playing cards?" he asked.

Casually, and without attracting any notice, Fernald studied the faces of the two men. At last, their features having been stamped on his memory, he turned to Garry, saying:

"Well, I'll know them if I ever see them again, but what of them?"

Hastily Garry related the instance of their conversing together in French, and their remark about the furs.

"We have planned that if they get off, Phil here will follow them, so that we won't lose track of them altogether. We are in hopes that they will eventually lead us to the fountain head of what we are seeking," he concluded.

"That would have been the wise thing to do in case you were alone," Fernald told them.

"But my being here with you changes the complexion of the matter somewhat. I think if they get off, it would be best for me to follow them. That is best for two reasons. Seeing the three of you together, would give rise to suspicions were one of you to detach himself suddenly from the rest and try to take up the trail of these men in their own town, for that is what it would be should they get off. Then there is another matter to be taken into consideration. Once let the smuggler band be caught, and only half of the job is done; the rest lies in finding the receiving point of these furs so that they may be seized, or the receivers be made to pay duty that they have evaded. Of course whoever is buying these furs knows they are shipped across the border as contraband. I shouldn't be a bit surprised if these men could lead me direct to something that would show where immense quantities of fur have gone in the past six months."

"I wonder where they are going to get off," remarked Garry.

"That is an extremely simple matter to ascertain. Why not look at the conductor's checks that are sticking out of their hatbands?" queried Fernald with a smile.

"Solid ivory," said Garry disgustedly, as he rapped his forehead sharply with his knuckles.

"Nothing to be ashamed of at all, old fellow," said Fernald easily. "It isn't to be expected that you should know all the tricks of the trade that you have known about not much more than a day. I've been doing this sort of work for twenty years now, and naturally many little bits of knowledge such as that are second nature to me, as natural as breathing or sleeping. Wait a minute while I go up and investigate."

Fernald got up, and acting as though his main idea was just to stretch his legs, strolled up to the front of the car. Passing the men, he stopped quite naturally to watch them play. When one of the men under observance took a trick with an exceptionally good play, he commented audibly on it. The man turned and smiled, showing his seat check as he did.

The system on the railroad was to give different colors for different stations. Fernald noticed that the checks of both men were of an identical color, and had the same number of holes punched in them.

After carelessly watching a moment or two longer, he returned and without stopping to speak to the boys, went past them and into the next car.

Here he engaged a brakeman in conversation, and at last returned to the boys, who were on tenterhooks to learn of his findings.

"I have found out that they are going to get off at the third station from here. However, we do not come to that for nearly two hours, so we have time enough to make any plans we need. I will follow them, and as soon as possible will come on to Hobart. However, when I get there, do not let on you know me, as we can be of infinitely more help to each other if it is not known that we are working together or even know each other. Whenever the need arises, I will find some way to communicate with you."

For the next hour or so, the conversation switched from one topic to another. Fernald was an interesting talker, and told the boys one or two of his adventures in the custom work of the United States.

Suddenly Dick slapped his leg and exclaimed excitedly:

"By George, our old friend the Hermit has no idea where we have disappeared to. I wish that we had had a chance at least to say goodbye to him and explain that we have been sent to a new station."

"Why not write him a note?" suggested Garry. "You can enclose it in one to Nate, asking him to deliver it the next time he goes into the woods to make an inspection trip. Mr. Fernald here will mail it for you when he gets off the train."

"That's a bully idea, Garry. Didn't have brains enough to think of it myself," chattered Dick.

"Never mind, old timer. Two heads are better than one you know, as the barrel said," laughed Garry.

Diving into his pocket, Dick drew forth the substantial notebook he always carried, and was soon busy writing a note, doing it as well as the jogging motion of the train would allow.

Finally he finished the note to the Hermit, and hastily scribbling one to Nate, enclosed the two in an envelope, addressed to the Deputy Ranger in Millinocket.

"There," he said, as he sealed the flap of the envelope. "Seems funny to be writing a note to the Hermit, doesn't it. The shoe generally used to be on the other foot when we were on the Patrol. By the way, there's one thing that's been puzzling me for some little time. What led you to think we were in any way connected with the same branch of work that you are, Mr. Fernald?"

"Oh, I'm no mind reader, or Sherlock Holmes," said Fernald with a hearty laugh. "It simply happens that I saw you in the Chief's office at Augusta, when I was there getting some final instructions. The Chief was going to introduce me, but I told him I preferred getting acquainted in my own way. To tell you the truth, at that time I thought the Chief had gone crazy, sending boys, but after looking you over, and unsuccessfully trying to pump you, I decided you boys had the right stuff in you, so made myself acquainted. Then too, I had a quiet bit of fun with you. Own up, now. Didn't you make up your minds that I was a suspicious character, especially after I had tried to get out of you what your business was?"

The boys looked sheepishly at each other, and then began to laugh.

"We must admit it, Mr. Fernald. We had you all ticketed as a person to keep a sharp eye on, until you gave the signal," confessed Garry.

"That's right, boys, one cannot be too careful. When you are on a mission of this kind, a mighty safe rule to follow is never to trust a person until he has unmistakably proven himself to be absolutely trustworthy. If you follow that rule, you'll never go wrong. Once in a while, of course, you'll find yourself in a position where you must use your own judgment. In that case, make sure you are dealing with a good patriotic American citizen, and you'll hit the key pretty nearly every time. Guess that little lecture will conclude our conversation for a while. We will be at the station where our friends disembark in a few minutes now, and I want to beat them to the door, so they will have no idea I am interested in their movements."

He got up and shook hands with the trio, and then in a loud tone, for the benefit of anyone that might be listening:

"Goodbye Boys, have a good camping trip and don't get lost in the Big Timber."

The boys echoed their goodbyes, and their new friend made his way to his seat where he unearthed a shabby old black traveling bag that appeared to have seen long and constant usage, as well as his blanket roll and rifle.

In the meantime, the card players had returned to their seat near that of the boys to get their luggage. They were chattering volubly in French, and Phil strained his ears, hoping to catch some additional clue, but their conversation was mainly about the pleasures of the trip they were just concluding.

"What are we going to do for supper?" inquired Dick.

"There! He's off again, Phil!" declared Garry. "It's only been four hours since he ate, and now he's thinking about supper."

"Well, four hours is four hours, and two more will make six, and persons should eat once every six hours. That's just human nature," protested Dick. He knew his chums were just ragging him, as they always did about his appetite, but he could never resist the temptation to argue with them, and protest that there was nothing abnormal about his capacity for food.

"I'm going back and find the conductor and see what arrangements have been made for feeding the hungry. And I'll bet a cooky you two are just as interested in the matter as I am," and Dick flounced out of his seat and went in search of the conductor. He came back shortly and announced they would stop an hour at the next town, about an hour's ride distant, for supper.

"Also they put on a sleeper there, and me for that. It beats sleeping in a day coach all hollow."

Came at last the station, and they hustled out to the little frame hotel that stood on the other side of the tracks. This town was more or less of a freight junction. They had a surprisingly good dinner, topped off with a famous New England pudding composed of Indian meal, baked, with grated maple sugar and pure cream poured on top of it.

Finishing the meal, they crossed the tracks back to the train. A sudden breeze lifted Phil's hat, causing him to chase it along the side of a string of freight cars. He stooped to recover it, looking under the freight car, as he did so. What he saw on the other side sent him back to his chums hotfoot.

"Say, fellows, don't think I'm just 'seeing things,' but those three tramps are sitting down there by the tracks eating!"

CHAPTER VII.

THE TRAIL BEGINS.

"Make a break for the train, boys," ordered Garry hastily. "We don't care to have them get a glimpse of us. I'll wager that they are making for the Canadian border, since as we know they have jumped their bail and are probably making for the national boundary line. Bringing them back will be a more difficult task than it would should they stay in the State of Maine."

"All I hope," remarked Phil, "is that they don't linger on the way, but keep right on going. The chances are that our search for the smuggling band will provide us with a new crop of people who are not especially friendly toward us, and old enemies will not be welcomed at the new headquarters."

The boys hunted up the conductor, and provided themselves with berths for the long night ride. They turned in early, for the adventures of the previous night had robbed them of some of their wonted sleep. Morning found them making their way through vast tracts of forest lands. The train made its usual stop at an eating place and the passengers disembarked for their morning meal. The boys hurried through the breakfast, in order that they might avail themselves of the remaining few minutes to make a hasty search of the train and vicinity of the depot to see whether or not the tramps were anywhere in the neighborhood.

The search proved unavailing, and they returned to their place in the smoking car, as the sleeper had been taken off at that station. The remainder of the ride for that day passed uneventfully. About the only topic of conversation was where they should make their headquarters when they arrived in their new location. They discussed the feasability of hiring lodgings in the town of Hobart, and after a short discussion discarded this plan, since it would not be in keeping with their characters as campers.

"My idea," explained Garry, "is to branch out from Hobart some little distance in the woods, and there for a time being, build a double lean-to.

The weather gives promise of being fair for some time to come, and if we find that circumstances warrant our staying in that vicinity, we can without a great deal of trouble build a pole cabin."

Late afternoon brought them to the town of Hobart, and cramped and weary from their thirty-six hour ride on the train, they gladly disembarked.

The little town of Hobart lay on the other side of the railroad tracks. It was like so many other small Maine towns, consisting of a huge general store, a smithy, which was also a garage, a great ramshackle building that was once a restaurant and a rooming house, evidently used by trappers who came there to dispose of their furs, and lumberjacks on their way to lumber operations in that vicinity. The boys proceeded directly to the general store, and here made inquiries as to the owner of the vast timber lands that entirely surrounded Hobart.

The shrewd old Yankee storekeeper told them that all the timber land in that section was controlled by one of the great paper and pulp companies of the State, and that campers never bothered to get permission to use the land.

Further inquiry brought out the information that the national boundary line was only about three miles from Hobart.

The boys decided to hike directly into the woods, build for themselves a fire, and sleep in the open, reserving the next morning to find a suitable camping place where they might erect their lean-to. They provided themselves with a week's supply of provisions, finding that they could come into town often enough to replenish their supplies as they ran out.

"Now," remarked Garry, after their provisions had been purchased, "we can do one of two things, either strike directly into the woods and cook our supper over a camp fire, or we can go over to the restaurant and have our meal there, which appeals most to me."

"I would suggest," said Phil, "that we eat tonight at the restaurant, not that I am too lazy to cook in the woods, but because it is probable that a good share of the people who live in this town, but who do not have real homes here, also eat there. In this way, we can become familiar at least with faces of those who inhabit the place, and who knows but what it may be the headquarters of the very crew that we are seeking."

"I think that's a prime suggestion," said Garry heartily, "so I move we leave our rifles and knapsacks here at the general store, and get our supper."

Before leaving they inquired from the storekeeper what would be the best route to take to bring them into the woods. They were told that to the eastward was a small farming community, and that the timber line did not begin in that direction for a matter of ten miles, but that to the southwest, a half-hour's walk, would bring them to the dense forests.

Making sure before they left their supplies at the store, that it would remain open until they had time to finish their meal, they repaired directly to the restaurant. Here they found a picturesque scene. A long counter ran the entire length of the room, presided over by an old French Canadian, clad in a red flannel shirt, rough corduroy trousers and high boots. To one side of the room were several tables, at which men were already seated, playing cards or checkers. A number of fine specimens of moose and deer heads hung from the walls.

The boys, perched upon high stools, were soon enjoying their meal. While they were eating, they kept their ears and eyes wide open, but their diligent attention brought them no reward. True, there were a number of rough looking characters about the room, who might have been members of or even heads of the particular band they had come to that country to find. The meal over, Phil wanted them to remain for a while, in the hope that some stray bit of conversation would give them something to work on, but Garry vetoed this idea, for the reason that there still remained only a half hour or so of daylight and he thought it would be wise for them to get to a point to make themselves a camp before darkness fell.

Retrieving their packs and rifles from the general store, they started for the woods, first filling their canteens, for it would probably be unlikely that they could find a spring immediately on their arrival. A half an hour's brisk walk brought them to the beginning of the timber line. The rapidly gathering dusk signalled the quick approach of nightfall, and they had barely penetrated the forest when Garry called a halt.

The first duty was to build a fire, and in a short time they had gathered enough brush to start their camp fire. A short search soon resulted in their finding an old fallen tree, and in a few minutes they had procured from this enough firewood to last them out the night. The last task before rolling in for the evening was to get a number of spruce boughs for making the usual mattress for anyone sleeping out in the open in the great forests of Maine.

Garry awoke with the dawn, and soon tumbled his companions out. Fresh wood was thrown on the few remaining embers, and in a short time coffee was boiling and bacon was being fried, while Dick superintended the making of a big batch of spider bread. It was the first meal that the boys had cooked over a camp fire in several days, and they heartily enjoyed every mouthful of it.

Breakfast over, the first task of the morning was to locate a suitable place in which to pitch their temporary camp. Striking out to the southwest, they spread out fanshaped, but not so far away that they could not hear the sound of each other's voices. Zigzagging back and forth, they searched for a spring. It was nearly a half of an hour before their search was rewarded with success, when Dick's call brought the three together.

Accidentally he had stumbled on an ideal camp site. It was one of those natural clearings that are so often found in the densest forests. Nearby was a clear spring, with cold water that trickled into an ever widening forest stream.

The boys immediately decided that a day's search might not have provided them with a better spot, and in a short time were bustling actively about building their new camp. This consisted merely of throwing together a brush lean-to.

The brush lean-to is the simplest sort of forest home. It is made by erecting two poles, six to seven feet in height, and about six to eight feet apart. In back of these, at a distance of some six feet, are placed two more poles about one-half the height of the first pair. Four poles are laid on the tops of these, secured by cutting a cleft in the tops, and laid so as to form the frame work for the roof of the lean-to. The next step in the building of such a habitation is to lay poles at an interval of a foot or a foot and a half along the roof part of the lean-to.

When erecting the uprights, care is taken to leave two or three bits of branch project at intervals along the length of the poles. On these long saplings are laid. The frame work of the lean-to is then complete, and the finishing step consists of cutting great quantities of brush.

These pieces of brush are hung on the saplings that have been spread across the frame work, the branches being crudely woven in and out of each other. The front of the lean-to is generally left open. Some woodsmen prefer to enclose all four sides, but the case of the brush shack being built by the boys, the front part was left open, since their idea was to build another lean-to directly opposite and about four feet away. In the open space between the two shacks could be built a camp fire.

The crude shacks thus constructed furnished them with ample protection during fair weather, and even during a moderate summer shower. Of course, in an extended rain, such shacks would be next to useless, as the steady downpour of rain would soon beat through the brush roof.

The shacks being completed, they chopped a quantity of firewood, using parts of fallen trees, wind wracked ruins that had dried and seasoned under the summer sun. This was stored away in one of the lean-tos. A balsam tree being found, quantities of the branches were cut to furnish beds for the three. The camp was now completed, and it being nearly noon, Dick departed into the woods to knock down a few squirrels for lunch. He was back in less than a half of an hour with three fat squirrels, and these skinned, impaled on a sharp stick, and wrapped with a slice or two of thickly cut bacon, were soon roasted over the red embers of the fire.

"Now, before we get down to business, who's for a trip to the border line? I want to see just how it feels to be in two countries at once," suggested Phil.

The boys agreeing, Garry drew out his pocket map and consulted it, bearing in mind the directions given them by the storekeeper. He decided they were less than five miles distant from the boundary, so striking out, they trudged steadily in what they believed was the proper direction. A walk of about an hour and a half brought them within what they considered was the proper location of the boundary line, then striking out toward the north-east, they spread out in search of one of the monuments or cairns that are erected at frequent intervals along border lines. Luckily, a few minutes' search brought them to one of the white stone posts which are common wherever two countries come together. On the top of the monument, chiseled in deep letters, were the words "Boundary Line." On the one side was cut "United States," while on the other was the word "Canada." Dick immediately straddled the post, exclaiming:

"Well, this is the first time that I have ever been in two countries at exactly the same moment." His enthusiasm was so infectious that Garry and Phil immediately followed suit and tried the novel experience.

Doubling back on the trail over which they had come, mid-afternoon found them back at their camp site. Here a surprise awaited them, for making free use of their coffee pot and one of their frying pans was a man, cooking a meal over their camp fire.

CHAPTER VIII.

THE GUM HUNTER.

"That chap seems to be making himself right at home in our camp, doesn't he, Garry," remarked Phil.

"So he does, but that is the way of many of the old timers in the woods. They consider it all right to make use of anyone's camp so long as they take nothing and do no harm, and leave some sign that they have been there, provided the owners do not return before he leaves. He's a picturesque-looking old fellow, isn't he? Looks something like our old Hermit friend. Let's go and see who he is," concluded Garry.

They made their way to the lean-to, for they had stopped when they saw the new occupant of the camp.

"Howdy, stranger," hailed Garry.

"Howdy, boys," he returned. "This your camp here?"

"Yes, we just threw it up yesterday. Are you from round these parts?" asked Garry.

"Callate that's just what I am. Name's Dudley, George Washington Dudley, generally called 'Dud' for short by my friends."

Garry then proceeded to tell his name and those of his companions. The old man left off his cooking long enough to shake hands, and then resumed his turning of the bacon.

"Got hungry and didn't want to start a new fire somewhere, and so used your place here. Wasn't expecting to be gone so long today, and didn't bring anything with me. Just helped myself. Will make it all right next time I come this way. What you boys doing up here? 'Spose you're from the city, but you don't look as though you were exact strangers to the woods. Sensible looking clothes you've got on, too."

"We're figuring on camping here for a time, and looking the country over. What's your business?" asked Garry, with the true Yankee inquisitiveness.

"Oh, I do several things. Just now I'm a gum hunter."

"A what?" chimed in Phil.

"Gum hunter," responded the old man briefly, as though that settled the question.

"I am afraid we don't know just what a gum hunter is," confessed Garry, speaking for his chums as well as himself.

"No, I 'spose you don't. Can't expect city boys to know a great deal anyway. Well, a gum hunter is just what it sounds like. I go through the woods getting spruce gum for the drug stores. Make a good living that way part of a year. Get a lot of druggists all way from Portland to Boston who won't buy spruce gum from anyone but me. They know I send 'em only the best. Understand what a gum hunter is now?"

"Thank you, yes," said Garry. "But you said you did other things. Mind telling us what they are? We are not inquisitive, only this is something new to us."

"Sure I don't mind. Sometimes I pick yarbs. There's a powerful lot of them in the woods, like sassafras root and checkerberry and things like that. I sell these to the same druggists that buy my gum. Then sometimes I guide parties. In the wintertime I trap. And sometimes in the spring, I work on the log drive on the river. There's lots of things a man can do to make a living in these woods, if he only knows enough. And it beats working in a store or something all hollow. You're never sick, and mainly you are your own boss, without anyone to tell you when to work and what to work at," concluded the old gum hunter.

For the benefit of our readers who may not be acquainted with Yankee dialect, yarbs is the native's way of saying herbs.

The boys were much interested in the old man's various occupations. They had no idea that a man could do so many different and profitable things in the wilds of the great forests.

"What you boys aim to do while you are camping?" inquired the newcomer, as he ate his late lunch. "You won't find a powerful lot of shooting as there ain't much now that the law is off. Course you can get some good fishing if you follow that brook that is fed by the spring you get

45

your water from for about three miles. There's a place there where a couple of old trees lay across the brook, blown down in some big storm, I expect, and there are some noble trout there. If I had had time today, I'd have gone down there and caught a couple for my meal, instead of taking your bacon."

"You were perfectly welcome to it, and anytime you are around here drop right in and help yourself. You'll always find a plenty," said Garry cordially.

"That's the right spirit to show in the woods, young feller," and the gum hunter slouched off to the spring to draw some water to wash the dishes after his meal. He came back with the water, and pouring a small quantity of it in the greasy frying pan, put it on the coals. The dish and his knife and fork, he scrubbed first with a handful of earth, and in a short time they were clean of the grease of the bacon. All that needed to be done was to rinse them out. By this time the water in the frying pan had come to a boil, and pouring it out, the pan was found to be nearly free of the grease. An application of earth, and a rinse, and that job was done.

Then filling an old pipe, he stretched out near the fire, and began to ply the boys with questions,—where they had come from, why they came so far from home to go camping, and countless other shrewd interrogations. For some reason he seemed to think it peculiar that they had come so far when there were plenty of forests nearer home where they could have established a camp.

Garry took it on himself to answer most of these questions, and in turn asked many of the old man.

Finally Garry looked straight at the old fellow, and asked quietly:

"Ever hear of any smuggling going on in these parts?"

"That's a funny question for a young fellow like you to be asking. You fellows haven't come up here to join some smugglers' band, that is, supposing there were any up here? Sure you boys haven't been reading woolly tales of smugglers on the border, or something, have ye?" he asked suspiciously.

Garry and the others laughed at the implication. Garry, although not so old in years, had several times proved himself to be a shrewd judge of character, and he had already made up his mind that the old gum hunter was a staunch and sturdy and patriotic citizen of the State. However, he decided to let a little time elapse before further questioning of the woodsman, or imparting any confidences to him.

"Where did your guide go after he fixed you up here?" asked the gum hunter, after a short silence.

"We didn't have any guide," answered Dick.

"You fellows mean to tell me that you picked this site and pitched camp yourselves?" demanded Dudley.

"Just exactly that," responded Garry.

"Well, it's mighty good job. Who taught you to make a double lean-to in that fashion?"

"Why, we've made rather a study of woodcraft, and this is not our first experience in the woods," answered Garry. Then thinking of a way in which he could let the old timer know that they were not merely adventurous, inquisitive boys, he decided to reveal to George Washington Dudley the fact that they were members of the Forest Ranger Service, but to keep a secret the fact that they were also on Customs duty.

On hearing this, the old man looked at them with considerably different aspect.

Garry explained to him, as it had been decided at Augusta to give them a good excuse for being in the woods, that they were covering that part of the country with a view to establishing a 'phone service for the Ranger System, that section being unprotected in that manner. As a matter of fact, the border line was but poorly guarded, as the meagre appropriation by the Legislature did not allow every foot of the country to be taken care of in the manner that it should.

This announcement by Garry increased the respect of the old man for them.

"Yes, sir, boys," he said, "that's one of the biggest things that's been done in this State for many a long year. I tell you, I've lived in these woods all my life, and that's more than sixty years, and I love these great trees. They all seem like so many friends to me. Of course I know that they must be sacrificed for the good of mankind, but it makes me sad when I think of the way the paper mill people have gone through mile after mile of timber land, cutting it clean of every tree. Course they should take only the big trees, that have grown old like men, and have almost outlived their good on earth. But to cut down young trees, it's just like killing young boys. To the paper mill people it only means just so much more pulp. Then the fires that are so often caused by careless campers and hunters. Yes, sir, it's sure a crime, and it's a fine thing for boys as young as you to know about these things and help fight the evils. But there's one thing that's been a puzzling me. What did you ask about smugglers for?"

"Why, it was partly curiosity, and partly because we heard that there was considerable smuggling in this part of the country, it being so near to the Canadian border line," said Garry cautiously. Then, carefully choosing his words, he went on:

"And if we did find evidence of any, we being in a branch of the State service, it would be our duty as good American citizens to run it down as far as possible and bring the smugglers to justice. Don't you think it would?" he concluded, looking sharply at old Dud.

"Yes sir," shot out the old gum hunter emphatically, and somewhat to the surprise of Garry, who had put the question merely to see what side the old timer would take. "I believe in upholding the laws of the land. I came from a family that has done that always. My Daddy fought in the Mexican War, and he was killed in Shiloh during the Civil War. I didn't tell 'em just the truth about my age in the Spanish War, and so I was in that myself; but they knew I was stretching the truth a little when I tried to get in the big scrap in 1917. Ain't never one of our family done anything but uphold the law the way she was written on the books.

"Now as for this smuggling that you speak of, it does happen and it happens right in this region. There's a regular nest of 'em right in Hobart.

Now mind I ain't saying anything, but if a person was to keep watch of certain fellows that always of an evening went through the back door at the end of the restaurant, he might some time know just who those fellows were. One thing, though, there ain't much help to be got from any of the townspeople when it comes to that practice. Lots of border people can't see the justice in paying duty on stuff that comes from a country that's as near them as Canada is. They don't seem to look on it as a foreign country at all. Guess it's because they are too familiar with it. And that's that. So now, boys, I'll bid ye a goodbye and trot along. I don't just know what you boys are up to, but I'll lay that it's all right, and I've just got this to say: Anytime you get into a bad hole, or need some help in the worst kind of way, remember and get to George W. Dudley, or old Dud the gum hunter. Everyone hereabouts knows who I am and where I can be found in a short time."

So saying, the old man shouldered his long rifle and went his way.

"Boys," said Garry elatedly, "the trail begins here!"

CHAPTER IX.

THE NIGHT VISITOR.

Night drawing on, the boys prepared their supper. The night's meal consisted of a real stew, for since they were so near to a place to purchase provisions they were able to indulge themselves a little more than when they were at their first station, so far away from a base of supplies.

Canned beef was used, and then a few potatoes and carrots were peeled and cut into small cubes. A good meat stew is one of the easiest things to make in the woods, provided one has a variety or two of vegetables.

All that is necessary to do is to cut the meat into small squares about an inch thick, then peel and cut the vegetables to the same size. Put just enough cold water in the kettle to cover the meat and vegetables, and then let the whole simmer slowly over the coals. From time to time the cook should take a look at the stew and see that it does not dry. It will be necessary to add a small quantity of water from time to time, and in about an hour and a quarter the stew will be ready, and after a long hike in the woods it is a dish that is fit for a king.

While Dick superintended the cooking of the stew, Phil and Garry replenished the wood supply. The stew put on the fire, Dick searched until he found a piece of sapling about an inch and a half in diameter. This is peeled off the bark and so made a rolling pin. A glass jam jar was then emptied of its contents and laid to one side.

"Ah, I perceive that we are going to have hot biscuits for supper tonight," remarked Phil, smacking his lips.

"Regular little Sherlock, aren't you?" said Garry with a laugh. "When you see a chap make a rolling pin and a biscuit cutter, you immediately reach the conclusion that he's going to make biscuits."

That was what Dick was intending to do. With a hot stew, there is nothing more palatable than a stack of piping hot biscuits cooked in a spider over a bed of red embers. They require but little work, only one thing being necessary, and that is to rub the shortening through into the flour. Many amateur campers wonder why the biscuits are flat or doughy. It is because they either do not know that the shortening should be ground in, or else, which is too often true, are too lazy to do the work.

For the benefit of some of our readers who may want to go camping over a summer week-end, the proper making of a pan of biscuits will be described. To make a dozen biscuits, or enough for three hungry boys, take a pint and a half of flour, a teaspoon and a half of baking powder, half a heaping teaspoonful of salt, the equivalent of a heaping tablespoonful of shortening, which may be bought by the can, (lard or drippings will do equally as well) and about half a pint of cold water. Stir the baking powder into the flour, then the salt. Then rub the shortening thoroughly into the flour, till not a bit of it remains in lumps or on the bottom of the mixing pan. Then stir in the water until you have a thick dough. In the meantime have a hot bed of coals, then dust a little flour on the bottom of one of your frying pans.

Finally roll out your dough with the home-made sapling rolling pin, and use an old glass jar or a small round tin to cut your biscuits out with. Knead over the bits that are left from cutting the biscuits out until all the dough has been used. Put them in the frying pan, and if you have no cover, use a second inverted pan for one.

Put this on the hot coals about twenty minutes before your supper is to be ready, and a few moments later put on the coffee pot.

The result will be a supper that cannot be found in the finest of hotels, especially if your appetite is sauced by a good hike and the fragrant balsamy air of the great forest.

Squatting about the glowing coals of the campfire, which cast a red reflection on the tall, sombre pines in back of them, they voted Dick a capital cook, and the supper one of the best they had eaten since they left the station where they had done fire patrol duty.

The meal over and the dishes washed, they discussed the advisability of establishing a guard as they had done when danger threatened them in past times.

Garry was of the opinion that it would be unnecessary for a time, as no one knew of their mission and they had seen nothing that would tend to alarm them.

The others were glad of this decision, for all were tired with the work of establishing the camp and the hike they had taken to the boundary line.

Shortly after midnight Garry was roused from his slumber by a nightmare in which he dreamed that LeBlanc and he were desperately battling on the top of a great cliff.

The dream was so realistic that when he woke, he shuddered for a moment. Then feeling somewhat chilly, he found that the fire had died down, and rose to throw a few sticks of wood on the still red coals. He cast a glance about him and in the distance saw a gleaming pair of eyes!

Hastily drawing his flashlight from his pocket, and diving back into the lean-to for his rifle, he made sure it was loaded and then investigated the gleaming eyes. His flashlight was a good one, throwing a long white beam of light into the darkness.

What he saw was some sort of an animal that, unperturbed by the light, was advancing slowly. Snapping off the flashlight, and dropping it to his side, he threw his rifle to his shoulder. He took a careful aim at a point between the shining eyes, and fired. There was a snarl and a violent squirming for a moment, and then all was still.

Garry's shot had sent the wild echoes chashing through the still forest, and in a trice, Phil and Dick were awakened, and came rushing to his side, bringing their rifles with them.

"What is it, Garry?" shouted Phil. "Have we been attacked?"

"No, but there is no telling what he might have done. As far as I could make out, it's a big bobcat. I haven't gone near it yet, for I am not sure that it is dead, although it hasn't made a move since I fired," answered Garry.

"Well, let's go and take a look. Load your rifle again, and we can keep ours trained on the beast and make short work of him if he is still alive," said Phil.

Garry rescued his flashlight from the spot where he had dropped it when he made ready to shoot, and the three started cautiously for the still carcass. Arriving at the point, Dick seized a dead stick from the ground and, throwing accurately, hit the animal in the ribs. It made never a move, and so the chums judged it was safe to approach.

The animal was stone dead. Garry's shot had pierced the brain right in the forehead, and the animal had evidently died almost instantly.

They examined the animal. It was a sort of a pepper-and-salt color with a pencil or streak of black hair extending from the back of the ears. As far as they could judge, it would stand about two feet tall, when erect, and must have been almost a yard from the top of its nose to the end of its abbreviated tail. The legs and feet were heavily covered with fur, and bore wicked, razorlike claws.

A snarl was on the face of the night prowler even in death. Garry seized it by the scruff of the neck, and hefted it.

"By George, I bet that animal weighs every ounce of thirty pounds," he exclaimed.

"Then it's the heftiest bobcat I've ever heard about," said Phil.

"Well, let's get back to bed again," yawned Dick. "I was sleeping like a log when I thought the whole shack had been pulled in about my ears. Good thing I woke up though. I forgot to put beans to soak last night, and I am determined to have baked beans for tomorrow night's supper. Guess I'll put them to soak and turn in again. Bring your old bobcat along and hang it to a branch, and we'll skin it tomorrow and try and tan it."

"Skin nothing," declared Garry. "I'm going to have that critter stuffed and mounted. It's one of the finest specimens I've ever seen."

"You fellows can argue all night if you want to," stated Phil emphatically. "I'm going to crawl into my blanket again. Good night!"

The boys returned to the camp, and still rubbing the sleep from his eyes, Dick put his beans to soak, and in a few minutes quiet had again descended on the camp, only the occasional snap of a burning knot breaking the majestic silence of the great forest that surrounded the sleeping boys.

When morning came, Garry was the first to awake. Glancing mischievously at his sleeping companions, he softly stole to where he had hung the body of the bobcat the night before, and hid it in the lean-to in back of the pile of cut firewood. Phil awoke a moment after, and coming out, looked for the animal to get a closer look at it in the daytime. He inquired in surprise where the carcass had gone.

"If you can keep a straight face and deny everything, we will have a few minutes of fun with Dick," said Garry with a wink.

"Go to it, I'm on," laughed Phil. Garry proceeded to start the coffee and slice the bacon for breakfast.

Then walking over to where Dick lay still soundly sleeping, he stirred him with his foot, shouting:

"Get up, lazybones, and make a mess of flapjacks for breakfast," for it was admitted by the boys that Dick was the best cook of the three.

Dick rolled out of his blanket with a protesting murmur, and then ran to the brook below the spring, where he dashed the cold water into his face until the sleep fog had rolled away. On his way back he glanced at the spot where the animal's body had been hung the night before. Not seeing it, he turned to Garry and asked what he had done with the wildcat.

"What wildcat?" asked Garry in amazement, while Phil looked at Dick with a blank face.

"Why, the bobcat or wildcat or civetcat, or whatever it was, that you shot last night."

Garry turned and shook his head sadly at Phil.

"Poor chap, the strain of the last few days has been too much for him, or else he is eating too much again before he goes to bed. He eats too much anyway, that's why he has such awful dreams."

"Dream nothing," shouted Dick, half angry, half puzzled. "Do you mean to stand there and tell me that you didn't turn the camp upside down last night by shooting some sort of an animal?"

"Absolutely," declared Garry firmly.

"That must have been some dream that you had last night," chimed in Phil, carrying out the joke.

Dick stared at his two companions, but seeing their sober faces, muttered something to himself and set about fixing the flapjacks. By this time he was firmly convinced that he had dreamed the whole occurrence, and on being pressed by the boys, told his "dream," relating exactly the circumstances of the adventure of the night before.

Although it nearly killed them to do it, the others maintained a straight face and listened with interest. Breakfast over, Dick was wandering around the camp when he discovered the beans he had set to soak when he was roused by the shot that killed the nocturnal visitor. Immediately he remembered that he had forgotten to do this before retiring, hence he must have done it when he got up.

Without saying anything to his companions, he quietly prowled about the camp, until he came on the body of the bobcat where Garry had hidden it. Instantly the light broke, and he made a dash for Garry, knocking him over and getting astride of him. Then Dick proceeded to tickle his ribs vigorously.

"Try to string me, will you? Holler nuff and say you're sorry you made fun of an innocent, trusting person like myself. Holler nuff."

"Hey, Phil, pull this wildman off me," gasped Garry between gasps of laughter, both at the tickling and at the recollection of the joke that had been played on the fat boy.

But Phil was rolling on the ground laughing until the tears ran down his cheeks. Both he and Garry had held in as long as it was possible, and now they were making up for lost time.

Dick at last tired of pummeling Garry, and soon he joined in the laughter, for the joke was undeniably on him.

While they were laughing, along came Dud the gum hunter, bearing a chicken with him.

"Here, boys, thought you might like a bit of chicken, and that'll help make up for the bacon and flour of yours that I used yesterday."

The boys thanked him heartily, and then Garry asked if he knew anyone in that region that could stuff a bobcat, explaining how he had shot one thenight before. Dud asked to see the animal, and then exclaimed, his eyes popping:

"Bobcat? Why, boy alive. That's the biggest, finest specimen of Canada Lynx I have even seen. It's one of the most savage animals to be found in the whole North Woods!"

CHAPTER X.

A SIGNAL OF DISTRESS.

"A Canada lynx!" ejaculated Garry. "Why, I thought they were to be found only in the wilds of Northern Canada."

"That's what a good many people think, but they can be found almost anywhere in the northern tier of this country. A friend of mine a couple of years ago shot one on the banks of Lake Champlain barely a mile outside the city of Plattsburg. I don't ever recollect seeing one as fine or as big as that one of yours. If you'd like, I'll stuff it and mount it for you."

"That is more than I dared hope," said Garry. "I didn't know whether I could find a taxidermist up here or not."

"You'll find that a good many old woodsmen are pretty skillful at it, especially those who hire out as guides in the deer season," replied Dud. "I mounted a fine deer head for a hunter from New York last year, and he said it was a better job than was done by one of the high-priced animal men in that city. But there's something else I want to tell you. I can't say much, but there is a pernicious lot of activity lately among a certain class of fellows who find a lot of business over the border every now and then. Now mind ye, I ain't saying anything, but I've seen and heard a couple of things since last night. Also, the 'lane' that is used by these fellows isn't a million miles from here, and a nod is as good as a wink to a blind mare. Remember I ain't said nothing at all."

Leaving the boys to ponder over his remarks, the gum hunter threw his bag across his shoulder and departed on his quest of spruce gum.

"Now I wonder why he is so secretive about this business. Evidently he knows all about it, so why shouldn't he come right out and tell what he knows. It's a puzzle," said Garry reflectively.

"Don't you suppose he is that way because he lives here and knows all these people and does not want to become involved in any way, fearing that they might seek revenge on him for giving away their secrets? Perhaps he even has some misguided relative or friend who is mixed up in the mess some way," suggested Phil.

"I believe that is the only solution, Phil. At any rate, it behooves us to be on the move and see what we can find out. He said something about thesmugglers' 'lane' being around here. I suppose that he means the trail over which the stuff is brought. I suggest that the business of the morning be to locate it if possible. Let's head toward the boundary stone, and strike up along what is approximately the border from there and see if we can discover anything in the way of a trail. First, however, I suggest that we take all our food supplies and cache them safely in a tree somewhere in this vicinity. Not so much for fear that they will be stolen, but because I don't want the fact advertised of our being here in case someone should come along in our absence. If we are here, then all right, if we are not, these lean-tos look to be only temporary, and no one would give them a second thought. I've also thought it would be a good plan to search out one or two other likely camp-sites and establish camps there. Then we can go from one to another and not advertise our presence so blatantly. So on our march today, keep an eye for a good spring. Now let's go and cache the stuff."

First Garry measured out a two-day ration of food, dividing it among the three. The rest was then packed in a cloth flour bag that Garry had procured at the general store, showing that he had had this idea in the back of his head since they had arrived at the border. Some little distance away, a thick pine tree was located and careful observation was made so that the boys could find it easily.

Phil climbed the tree and then let down his lariat and Garry tied the bag to the end. Phil then drew it up into the tree and placed it securely in a crotch in one of the branches. This done, Phil clambered back down, remarking when he reached the ground:

"If we get a good storm it's goodbye to the sugar and flour in that bag. The stuff will just naturally melt away. If we are going to make a practice of caching the stuff, I suggest that we provide a number of tin cans with tight covers. Then it can rain on the articles for days and never hurt them a bit."

"That's a prime idea, Phil, and next time we go to town, you are delegated to provide said tins," said Garry.

"Ha, that's the time I talked myself into extra work," rejoined Phil with a laugh.

"Believe me, young man, I'll take a lesson from that and make only suggestions that won't entail extra work," chipped in Dick.

"On our way now, but first Dick, you run back to the camp and empty your canteen on the fire, and obliterate all traces of it. Then fill your canteen and rejoin us here, and we'll be off for the boundary monument," ordered Garry, thus proving himself to be a real woodsman and Ranger, never forgetting that a stray spark or ember may smoulder for some little time and perhaps start a fire that would sweep through the forests as though they were so much tinder.

Dick sped away to do Garry's bidding, and in a few moments was back, and the three chums started for the boundary line. This time they were able to proceed directly to it, without wasting precious time hunting for it.

Arriving at the marker, they branched out fanshaped as was their wont when they were in search of a trail or water. For some three or four miles they found nothing in the way of a well-defined trail, or even the remains of a camp, and were beginning to think the whole affair was nothing more nor less than a wild goose chase, when they were called together by a hail from Dick.

They ran speedily to him, and found him gazing at the ground.

"I don't know that what I've found amounts to a continental, but this is an old abandoned tote road, and I've found the marks of three or four different style boots, or rather, different sized boots. To my mind, it is worth following up, as there hasn't been anything yet worth while investigating except this. I wonder if our friend Dud isn't just giving us a wrong steer, or is this what he meant we should find? What say, Garry, what shall we do?"

Garry decided immediately.

"We'll follow this for a bit and see where it leads us. It may amount to nothing at all, and then again it may lead us to a real clue."

They set off down the old tote road, and after a walk of nearly an hour came upon several shacks, all boarded up, and bearing an air of desolation and abandonment.

"By golly, this is a deserted lumber camp. You remember the storekeeper told us there used to be logging operations in this vicinity? This must have been the scene of the camp, although they had quite a haul to reach the river for the drive. Let's take a look-see and find out what's here," cried Phil.

They went to the main building, that is, the largest, evidently what had been the bunkhouse for the lumberjacks, but every window was tightly boarded up. A little to one side was a smaller building, which had probably been the office and home of the camp boss and timber cruisers, who generally lived by themselves.

This, too, had a deserted and forlorn appearance. Phil's keen eyes were roving over the ground, but he found nothing to excite him till he came to the rear of the building. Here was a small door.

"Say, fellows, look at that door. It's been repaired, and only lately. You can see that someone has tried to obliterate the fact that new boards were put in. It looks as though some tramp or woods wanderer had broken in at some time, and the person or persons who have been here lately have repaired it," said Phil, dropping to his knees and examining the ground in front of the door.

"Why might not whoever has charge of this camp have fixed the door? It is very likely that when the logging operations were given up that some person in Hobart was put in charge to see that it was not destroyed, because logging can again be carried on in this section," inquired Dick.

"Why, I dope it out this way. If, as you say, there is a caretaker or an agent, it would be only natural for him to repair the broken door; but why take all the trouble to smear it with dirt and dent it a little to make it appear that it hadn't been touched? You can see that there are different woods used in the door, and the repaired part is of much newer timber. I tell you, there is some reason for this secrecy. By Jove, let's try and get in."

As he spoke, Phil ran to one of the windows. This had been boarded up from the outside, but one of the boards appeared to be loose.

"What say, Garry, shall I try and make an entrance?"

"I think under the circumstances it would be all right, since we are in search of possible evidence," replied Garry, after a moment's consideration.

Carefully inserting the edge of his axe under the loose board, Phil worked the axe handle slowly, until at last he was rewarded by the board giving way, gently withdrawing the nails with it. In a few moments more, he had a second board removed, disclosing a window. It had an ordinary lock, and opening his knife, Phil inserted the blade and soon snapped the lock back. In a few seconds the three had clambered in, and were taking stock of the interior.

Undeniably the place had been recently occupied. On the table were two bottles with the remains of candles stuck in them, while in the fireplace were the remains of a fire. A good woodsman can tell whether a fire has been made recently or not, and the boys saw at once that this was the case.

On the table was a pack of cards, thrown there evidently at the ending of a game. There were four bunks at one side of the room, and these had been cleaned out and fresh boughs were laid there, although there were no blankets.

Garry discovered a closet, and on opening it, found that there was a fair stock of provisions.

"Guess you are right, Phil. Someone is making a headquarters of the shack. It seems logical to think that they are doing so secretly, for if anyone with a right to use the place were living here, they would have removed the boards from the windows, and would have made the place a little bit morehabitable. However, we had better dust out of here, for we don't want to be surprised by anyone that happens to come along, especially whoever is using this place. Perhaps it would be a good idea to establish a watch and see who comes here. The chances are whoever uses the place comes at night, or at least in the early evening, and one might be able to get a look at them. At any rate, let's hike out," concluded Garry.

Looking around carefully to see that they left no evidence of their surrepticious visit, they went out through the window.

"Sorry there's no way to lock that window hasp again, but since the windows are evidently not used by the occupants, I don't believe it will ever be noticed," remarked Phil, as he carefully nailed the boards back in place with the back of the hatchet, being careful that his axe did not slip and leave a mark to show that the boards had been pried off.

"When it comes time to watch for the occupants, I have an idea of the proper place to keep an eye on them," said Dick, "and that is the spring. Whoever is living here must have water, and if I'm not mistaken, that's the spring over there."

Following Dick's lead, they went in the indicated direction, and sure enough, there was the spring.

"You can see fairly fresh footprints there. I wish now that we had Sandy with us," said Garry.

"Sandy" was Garry's big Airedale dog, which they had left with Nate Webster when they went off to Augusta. They had not taken him on the trip, for all those with whom they had had trouble, knew the dog, and he would call too obviously attention to the presence of the trio of Rangers.

"Let's take a look at the big bunkhouse and see if that is being used also," suggested Phil.

They returned to the long low shack, and were in search of a window from which the boards might be removed, when suddenly Garry said:

"Listen, do you hear the sound of rifle shots?"

Faintly borne on the breeze, came the sound of a distant shot.

"Probably only some youngster from town out after rabbits," said Dick. They waited for a few minutes, and then again was heard a shot, closely followed by two more.

"The forest distress signal. Some one's in trouble boys!" cried Garry excitedly.

CHAPTER XI.

THE RESCUE.

To explain to our readers why the three shots are known as a distress signal is simple. One shot would ordinarily be that of a hunter. Two could be the same thing, provided the man was using a double barrelled shotgun, such as is used in hunting birds. The chances that a hunter would fire three shots in regular succession is very small, hence this is the signal that is the S. O. S. of the woods. It is reported at intervals, and after being heard two or three times, the woods voyager may be sure that someone is in some great difficulty, fallen and broken a leg, or lost in the dense timber.

"It's to the south of us," said Garry, as he wet a finger and held it up to test the direction of the wind. "You see the breeze comes from that direction, and the sound comes with it. Let's take it on the trot, boys."

So saying, he led the way at an easy lope to the southward. They had proceeded a little distance, when again they heard the three shots, this time much nearer.

Breaking into a swift run, they were soon at the source of the call for help.

Laying on the ground, his foot caught in a wicked looking steel trap, was an elderly man. In a feeble tone, he hailed the boys.

"Thank God you've come, boys. I fear in a little while more I should have been too weak to try and summon help. Release me from this trap."

Garry and Dick sprang to the trap, which had closed on the man's ankle, while Phil attempted to lift him up.

"Easy, my boy, easy, my arm's broken. That's why I was unable to release myself sometime ago. I could only reach one spring with my good arm, and even that effort so twisted my leg that I fainted and had to give up attempting it."

While he had been speaking, the two boys had released the springs, and bending back the teeth, released the man's leg. He gave a groan of relief, while trying to raise himself up.

"Better take it easy, sir, while I look you over and see what the extent of your injuries are," said Garry.

Taking his knife, the boy slit the leg of the corduroy trousers, and then carefully rolled the woolen sock down. This disclosed an ugly looking swollenleg. Very gently he felt of the leg, and then asked the man if he could move his foot. After trying, the old man found he could.

"Guess it's not broken, just very badly bruised and swollen," remarked Garry cheerfully.

"That's something to be thankful for anyway, for I know my arm is broken. It was all I could do to load and fire my rifle with one hand," said the sufferer.

"We'll have that in splints in no time, and then see about getting you to your home," said Garry. "Now Phil, you start a little fire and make some coffee to brace the gentleman up with, while I put his arm in splints."

Very gently he ran his fingers up and down the arm, finding that it was a clean break of one of the bones of the forearm, and not the wrist. Searching through his knapsack, he drew out what is known to first aid as a wire gauze bandage. This is nothing more than closely meshed wire, and is recommended for use for a temporary splint until the doctor can be gotten.

Wrapping the arm with some bandage, he put on the splint, and tied it on firmly with a strip of bandage. Then whipping his bandanna handkerchief from around his neck, he made a sling.

The hot coffee was soon forthcoming, and stimulated by it, the man felt considerably better.

Asked how he had been caught by the trap, he explained that while he was walking through the woods in search of a partridge or squirrel, mainly more for the pleasure of hiking than in hope of shooting anything, he had stepped into the trap, which was carefully covered.

"It had evidently been there for some time, for the ground over it looked quite natural as though many successive rains had beaten down upon it, or else I would have noticed that the covering was only artificial. By the way, let me introduce myself. My name is John Everett, and I used to be the Customs officer here, until Uncle Sam decided there was no need for one, and moved the station some twenty-five miles up the border, where another man, a politically influential fellow, was appointed to the new office. Since then I have been living in retirement with my granddaughter. I wonder if it is going to impose on you to ask one of you to go to Hobart, it's only about four miles from here, and get help to take me home, for although my leg does not seem to be broken, I cannot stand on it, much less walk," he concluded.

"Don't worry about getting home. We'll have a snack of food and then make a stretcher and have you there in no time," said Garry.

"I am afraid that will be too much of a task for you," remonstrated Everett.

"Oh, it's nothing at all, sir," Garry hastened to say.

When the man had mentioned that he had been a Customs officer, Dick had given Phil a significant glance. There was every chance that good fortune in being able to do a great favor for the old man might redound to their aid.

A hasty lunch of bacon and spiderbread was made, the man watching admiringly the efficient and speedy manner in which the boys went about preparing the meal.

"You boys act as though you had been born and brought up in the woods. Were you?" he inquired.

"No, although we have always liked woodcraft and forest lore, and have read about it and practiced it in a small way. We are in the Forest Ranger service, doing some special work, and so we have to know something about it," answered Garry.

Lunch over, the effect of the food on the old man being to cheer him up and strengthen him, the fire was stamped out, and then Phil and Dick proceeded to make a litter while Garry cut two strong, tough saplings to make the handles.

They made the litter by taking off their coats and buttoning them securely. Then the coats were turned inside out, so that the arms were inside the jackets. Through the arms were thrust the two saplings, which had been cut sufficiently long to allow them to project a foot and a half or so beyond the two coats. A blanket was then laid atop the coats, and the litter was ready.

Dick and Garry took the first turn at carrying, while Phil went ahead carrying the rifles. Every few moments, the third boy would relieve one of the others. Frequent rests were necessary, and they were not able to make much more than a mile an hour, so that it was late afternoon when they finally reached the outskirts of the town.

"There's my home there, the white house set back in from the street," said Everett. "I am afraid you boys are rather tuckered out."

As a matter of fact they were, for the four-mile hike with the burden on the litter was no mean task.

They had hardly turned in the gate, when a pretty girl of about seventeen or eighteen rushed out to meet them. When she saw her grandfather on the stretcher, she turned pale, and in anxious voice asked what the matter was.

"Don't be alarmed, Ruth, I just had a little accident in the woods and broke my arm. Otherwise I'm fit as a fiddle. Now don't worry, and hold the door open for these young men to carry me in and then run over and get Dr. Mills."

Once in the house, Mr. Everett was laid on a couch and made as comfortable as possible for the time being.

"This is my granddaughter, Ruth," he told the boys. "In the excitement of the day, I quite forgot to ask your names, so you will have to introduce yourselves to her."

This Garry, acting as master of ceremonies, did, and then the girl hastened after the doctor. She returned with him in a few minutes, and the physician promptly began his examination.

He confirmed Garry's finding that the leg was not broken, and complimented him on his neat job of putting on the temporary splint. Since the break was simple, and the old man protested that a little twinge of pain was nothing, the arm was immediately set and the permanent splints set in place.

The chums assisted the doctor to get Mr. Everett to bed, and then bade him goodbye, promising to look in very soon to see how he was getting along.

"Don't fail to call on me, boys, if I can be of any service to you," were his parting words.

"Well, sir, we may do that very soon," said Garry.

"You'll find that I won't fail you," promised Everett.

As they were on their way out, the girl stopped the chums and expressed her gratitude for their rescue of her grandfather.

"I don't know how to thank you boys. Just think, if you hadn't come along, he might have died out there in the woods before someone found him, and he is the only relative I have. I am sure there is nothing I wouldn't do for you that was within my power," she declared.

"Do you really mean that, Miss?" said Garry.

"Indeed I do. Just let me know what I can do," she answered eagerly.

"I don't want you to think I am asking this as a matter of reward," said Garry, "but it's something that is very vital to the success of our mission here. I feel that we can be frank with you, since your grandfather was once in the Customs service. I can't explain just now how we are connected with the matter, but you could do us and the State a great service if you could tell us if you know anything about smuggling operations here. You are practically the only one that we have given so much confidence, and I am sure that you will respect it."

"Oh, of course I will. I don't know who or what you are, but I am sure you are all right. As for what you ask, I don't know much about it, although Granddaddy has confided his suspicions to me many times. Unfortunately, though, they are only suspicions, and he has never been able to get any tangible evidence, for they cover their tracks very cleverly, and especially with him, since they know that he was once in the service. I can tell you this, though, keep sharp watch of a man called Lafe Green. He is a great big red-haired man, and he hangs around that restaurant that is run by a man called Joe Canuck. It's practically the only one in town, perhaps you know of it."

"We do know of it, and we sure thank you for what you have told us, and you will never regret it. Sometime we can tell you more about all this. I hope we shall see you again, for we will come at the first opportunity to see how your grandfather is getting along," said Garry, as the three took their leave, bidding goodbye to the pretty girl.

Out on the street again, Dick could scarcely restrain himself from doing a war dance on the sidewalk.

"Gosh," he ejaculated exuberantly. "Talk about casting your bread upon the waters and having it come back a whole shipload of angel cake. This is luck. Boys, at last we're on the track of the smugglers, and if the firm of Boone, Durant and Wallace doesn't run them down, I'll go back home and spend the rest of the summer working in a grocery store or on a farm pulling weeds!"

CHAPTER XII.

THE COMING OF THE BEAR.

"Listen fellows, let's duck back towards the woods for a bit and have a council of war," ordered Garry. "There will be less chance of our being observed there, and no chance of our being overheard." So saying, Garry led the way back for about half a mile.

"We must strike while the iron's hot, and it seems to be hot tonight. What with the young lady's information about watching this Lafe Green person, and Dud's hint that there was something brewing, it strikes me that we ought to get going. There's only one logical place to start, and that is this restaurant," said Garry emphatically.

"We must understand one thing, though. There's an element of danger connected with this, and I don't want to lead anyone into anything that I wouldn't do myself, so I offer to make the first reconnoitre," he concluded.

"That's mighty white, Garry, but I want to make a suggestion. I'm not looking for any personal glory out of this, but I declare I think I am the logical person to go. You know I am the only one of us who can talk French and understand it, and as we have already had one clue in that manner, there's every chance that others may follow in the same way, so I move that I go."

Garry saw the force of the argument, and as Phil was backed up by Dick, decided that after all this was the best move.

A plan of campaign was hastily drawn up. It was decided that the other two should return to the lean-to, and there wait Phil's return. Phil's rifle and knapsack were to be carried back by his chums, while Phil was to take the little automatic that Garry had purchased at Bangor.

"This is only as a measure of safety, Phil," said Garry. "And under no condition show it or use it except as a last resort. Now there's one other thing. We want to keep a check for safety's sake on your movements, yet you want to have time enough to follow up any clue that may arise. So let's make it a point that you be back at the lean-to by sundown tomorrow night. If you are not there by then, we will know that you are in some sort of a pickle and plan to come to your aid. Don't try to do anything single handed; your mission tonight is to find out what is going on if you can. If you can return tonight, so much the better. From now on too, we'll establish a watch, taking two hour sentry duty. There may be no need of it yet, but we will get back in the habit of it, and an ounce of precaution is worth a pound of cure. Now go to it, old topper, and the best of luck."

The chums shook hands, and then went their different ways, Garry and Dick back to the lean-to in the woods, and Phil back to town.

Just before he left the fringe of woods that bordered the edge of the town, Phil did a peculiar stunt that was later to stand him in good stead. Taking his knife from his pocket, he made a small slit in the under side of his coat lapel. In this he slipped the knife, and then held the coat at arm's length to see if there was any lump observable. The coat, made as it was of thick khaki, showed no noticeable difference. Satisfied with the appearance, he slipped his coat on again, and went his way. Phil was thinking of the time he had been left chained to the tree in the woods by Anderson and LeBlanc, with no weapon with which he could free himself, and he was determined that this would never happen again if he could prevent it. He was satisfied that the ruse of hiding the knife would not be discovered were he captured, unless his coat was taken away from him.

In a short time Phil had approached the restaurant, and entered. Taking his seat on one of the high stools at the lunch counter, he ordered some supper. The bearded Frenchman, evidently the proprietor, who approached, shot at him a question in French.

Phil know perfectly well that he was asking him in French what he wanted, but he just stared blankly at the man, who, believing that he did not understand, spoke to him in broken English.

"M'sieu does not spik the French, hein?"

Phil shook his head and repeated his order in English. Satisfied, the man turned to the stove back of the counter and dished up a mess of piping hot baked peas, cooked with bacon instead of pork. This is a favorite dish with the French of Canada. A great slab of johnny-cake and a cup of hot coffee seemed to be the only thing on the bill of fare. For dessert there was apple pie and cheese.

The whole was put before him at once, and Phil, with the appetite of a healthy boy, fell to and soon dispatched the food. He ate a second portion of the peas, which evidently pleased the proprietor who was at once cook and waiter.

Following the order for the second helping, the big Frenchman entered into conversation with Phil. He seemed satisfied with Phil's answer to his query as to what he was doing in those parts, when Phil told them he was camping there for a short time, preparatory to a fishing expedition.

Supper over, Phil walked over to one of the tables, where he found a week-old Bangor paper, and a Canadian French paper. Carefully avoiding taking up the French paper and thus betray his knowledge of the language, he took the Commercial and read steadily for an hour or more. During this time the place was steadily filling. Men came in, got their supper, and took seats at the many tables scattered about. Later others came in, evidently villagers who made a sort of a clubhouse of the place. A half a dozen card games were in progress, and at three of the tables couples were playing checkers. By this time Phil had read all the news and was beginning on the advertisements in order to have some ostensible purpose in remaining where he knew nobody. Another half hour passed, and then he decided to get up and watch one of the checker games that was in progress near him.

Both of the players were fairly expert, and he watched for some time with great interest. During the second game, one of the players made a bad move and let his opponent sweep off three pieces and land in the king row to boot. As he made the move, Phil could not repress a little gasp. The lucky opponent looked up at Phil and grinned, and Phil smiled back. The game was lost for the first man, and his friend proceeded to rub it in a little.

"I declare, Hoke, you're gettin' worse every day. You ought to see that I would clean the board if you made that move. I declare, I bet this young fellow here can beat you."

"Bet a doughnut he can't," said the man called Hoke.

"Take ye up on that, an' if you lose I'll make you walk home and get one. They never have 'em here at night. What say, young feller, will ye give this feller a trimming for me?"

"Why, yes, I would like to play a game," said Phil. He wanted to play for two reasons. First, it would give him a legitimate excuse for loitering there a little longer without attracting attention, and secondly, he really enjoyed a good game of checkers.

Phil disposed of his man very easily, for he was a remarkably good player. At the conclusion of the game, the defeated man demanded that his friend try a game with Phil, and accordingly changed places with him. Here was a harder opponent, and Phil was devoting his entire attention to giving him a run for the honors of the game, when the door opened and a couple of men slouched in.

Phil's heart stood still, for they were two of the trio of tramps they had caught in their shack outside their home town. Phil was in a quandary. He couldn't leave the game and rush out of the restaurant without doing the very thing he least wanted to, that was draw particular attention to himself.

There was only one thing to do, and that was stay and face the music. He doubted if the tramps would start anything in the room, but would probably wait outside and seek to wreak revenge on him for being one of those instrumental in their capture that time in the shack.

Then to his great surprise, they passed by him, giving him only a casual glance, but no sign of recognition.

Phil breathed a sigh of relief, and then reflected that it was not strange that they failed to recognize him. In the first place, they would hardly expect to find him in that northern town, and then his khaki clothes were of the sort that is common to the woods, but not to the town where their arrest had taken place. So it was a simple matter, their not knowing him.

He turned his attention to the game again, and had made two moves, when a phrase, spoken in French by a man at the table in back of him, startled him into alert attention.

The man had said:

"Well, Pierre, 'The Bear' will be here in a few moments now."

What was he to do? "The Bear" could be no one but LeBlanc.

He must get out of the room at all costs, but how was he to avoid running into LeBlanc?

There was precious little chance that the guide would fail to recognize him, and he knew that he would be in real danger here among the half-breed's friends and cronies.

Then, too, he must make his exit naturally, so as to arouse no suspicion in the minds of the checker players, who might be foes just as well as friends.

Already the watcher at the table was demanding they finish the game quickly so that he could have another chance at Phil.

His mind working rapidly, Phil figured out what the best course to pursue would be. The main point was to get out of the restaurant, but there was the danger that at the precise moment of his exit, Jean LeBlanc might be coming in the door.

It was not wholly fear of LeBlanc that made him want to escape unobserved, he didn't want the treacherous guide to know that he or his chums were in the vicinity, for it would immediately destroy their usefulness; at least it would hamper their work to a great degree.

While his opponent studied the board, Phil was looking about the room. At one side of the room there was a window looking out on a side street oralley, Phil did not know which. Right beside it was a door. He decided that this was the best means of exit, for in the dark alleyway he could pass anyone coming in without their seeing who it was, and once in the shadows, he could look up and down the street, and make his escape as soon as it looked clear.

The immediate thing to be done was to bring the game to a close. His opponent had made his move, and concentrating on the game, Phil saw an obscure move, which, once made, would give his opponent the game. Without further hesitation, he made it, and the other player seized the advantage and won the game.

While he was chuckling over his victory, the other man was demanding a return chance at Phil, but the Boy Ranger forestalled this by pleading a headache from the heat and the smoke-filled room.

"Tell you what," he said. "You two play a game, while I go outside for a few minutes and clear my head, then I'll come back and take you on again."

This proved to be agreeable to the others, and in another moment they were absorbed in the start of the game. Carefully edging his way over to the side door, he waited till no one was looking at him, then opened the door and slipped through — not into an alleyway, but into another room!

He had been fooled by the close proximity of the window, never dreaming that there was an ell-like extension beginning flush at the side of the window. Hastily glancing about, he saw another door, and running to it, threw it open, only to have Jean LeBlanc enter just as he opened it.

CHAPTER XIII.

TRAPPED.

Phil's hand darted to his pocket for the automatic that Garry had given him before he started on his mission, but he was not quick enough, for in less than an instant LeBlanc had leaped upon him, pinioning his arms to his side. Phil was helpless in the grasp of the half-breed. LeBlanc called in French for help, and in another moment the black moustached proprietor came rushing in.

While LeBlanc held Phil, Canuck searched his pockets, taking from him what little money he had, and the automatic revolver. Evidently suspicious that Phil might have some other weapon concealed about him, they made him unlace and take off his shoepacks; here, of course, they found nothing, but fortunately they did not notice the secret pocket that he had made in the lapel of his coat, in which reposed safely his heavy scout knife.

In the meantime, the French restaurant proprietor and LeBlanc carried on a swift conversation in French, all of which, of course, Phil understood perfectly.

"We shall take him up to the room on the third floor that we know about, and keep him there until we shall have decided what to do with him."

Phil was unceremoniously hustled out through the rear door, and with a couple of brutal shoves, was taken up the dark stairway. Still, a second flight he went up, and was then drawn into a dark room. Just before they closed the door upon him, his heart sank, as he heard LeBlanc tell the proprietor:

"This is the fourth time that I have met this boy. He seems fated to work me harm. Once I left him for dead in the Great Woods, but he seemed to have a charmed life and escaped. This time, I promise you he will not."

So saying, they slammed the door, and Phil heard the rasp of the heavy lock being turned in the door. Groping his way about, he found that the room was bare of all furnishing, except for a decrepit old cot, and a rough table. Feeling for the top of the table, he discovered there was an old bottle, with a good-size piece of candle in it. He went through his pockets carefully to see if by chance his searchers had left behind them a stray match, but his hunt was not rewarded.

There was nothing to do but make the best of the darkness. He groped his way to the cot and sat down, taking stock of the situation. There seemed to be nothing he could do except to wait for the morning, provided that he would be allowed to see the morning come, then to look about the room in search of some method of escaping. Thanks to his foresightedness, he still had his knife, and this might prove to him to be salvation as far as escape was concerned. He laid down on the cot, thinking, and after nearly a half of an hour jumped to his feet, inwardly calling himself names for his forgetfulness.

Not until that moment had he remembered that he generally carried several matches, wrapped in a bit of oil silk and tucked under his hat band. It was a trick that Garry had taught him when they first went in the woods.

Fumbling inside of the hat band, he came upon a little package of half a dozen matches, still securely wrapped in the oiled silk in which he had placed them, almost a month before.

"What a fool I was," he muttered to himself. "All that time that I was tied and chained to a tree by LeBlanc and Anderson, I had those matches and never once thought of them."

So saying, he carefully struck one of the matches and lighted the candle. He now had a chance to examine the prison room that he was in. Save for the door, the only other means of egress from the room was a solitary window, but a quick examination showed that escape in this way was impossible, for the shutter of the window, instead of being composed of wood was made of a solid piece of iron.

Phil then examined the door, finding that this was evidently made of several thicknesses of hard wood, so thick was it, that when he rapped strongly with his knuckles, it gave forth a dead heavy sound, showing that it was unusually thick. It was so thick and hard, in fact, as to defy any effort to cut it through with his knife. Phil hardly knew what to do; all way of escaping seemed barred to him.

There was one chance, however, and that was a possibility of attacking whatever guard came to bring him food in the morning, for he did not believe that they intended to starve him to death.

Grasping the bottle that held the candle, he went over and made an examination of the cot. It was an old folding cot, made of fairly heavy cross braces, bound with substantial pieces of metal.

Phil unshipped his knife from the coat lapel cache, and immediately set to work to whittle away one of the cross pieces that supported the cot. He whittled in such a fashion that on one end remained one of the iron braces, screwed securely to the stick of wood. Hefting it in his hand, and then swinging it about his head, Phil discovered that he had a weapon that would almost fell an ox. His plan was to wait beside the door in the morning until whoever brought him his food should have unlocked the door, then to strike him down, and while he was stunned, take a chance on escaping from the house.

The broken cot did not offer a very comfortable sleeping place, but Phil propped it up the best he could and lay down upon it. It was too rickety, so stripping the tattered blanket from it, he lay upon the floor.

This was no hardship to him, as he had spent many a night of his life sleeping upon the hard, solid earth, which is not a whit softer than a flooring made of pine boards.

As he lay dozing, he almost fancied that he could hear a very low murmur of voices. Telling himself that it was only his imagination, he rolled over again and tried to sleep, but the excitement and the uncertainty made him sleepless. Again he heard a low mutter of subdued voices, then he sat straight up in his blanket.

Since he could not sleep, he felt that he might as well be busying himself about something, so drawing a blanket over to a corner of the room, he laid down flat upon it, and with the drill punch on his scout knife, began to bore a hole in the floor. He remembered that the ceiling of the restaurant was made of boards and not of plaster, and he decided that this was probably the case all through the rest of the house. There was probably a double thickness of boards, and the longer he drilled the more certain he became of this.

Finishing, he could feel that he was within the merest fraction of an inch of piercing the double thickness of boards, through which he had carefully bored his way. Instead of piercing his knife blade straight through the thin bit of board that was left, he began to enlarge the hole that he had already made. When he had done this to his satisfaction, he blew out the candle, for he wanted no stray gleam of light to betray to whoever was in the room below him his course of action.

Having extinguished the light, very carefully and slowly, he dug away tiny splinters of the thin bit of board that separated him from hearing, and perhaps seeing, what was taking place in the room below. As he made the hole, the murmur of voices became more and more distinct. At last, the sharp point of the knife pierced the board, and then working as carefully as though he were handling the most deadly explosive, he began to enlarge the little chink that he had made.

Having completed his peep hole, he glued his eye to it, but was unable to make out anyone in the room below him. Evidently, the occupants of the room were outside of his field of vision. Giving up trying to see what was going on, he lay on his side with his ear pressed closely to the aperture that he had made. He could distinguish LeBlanc's voice, also that of the French restaurant proprietor. There seemed to be two other men in the room, for he could make out the difference in voices, but they were strangers to him. Evidently, the two strangers could not speak French, for LeBlanc and the proprietor were talking in English.

Phil could hear the conversation as plainly as though he were sitting in the room with them. As soon as he discovered what they were talking about, he became very much excited, for they were discussing the details of a fur smuggling trip that was to take place that very week. Phil thought to himself, that if he could only get out of the prison room, he had the most valuable clue that he or his chums had yet discovered. He thought it strange that they made no remark about the deserted logging camp, for

Phil was certain that this was the headquarters, or at least a rendezvous, of the smuggling band.

Phil had wondered that he had seen or heard nothing of Anderson, for he expected wherever LeBlanc would be, the other would be found also. However, from the conversation he learned that Anderson had already crossed the border line, and was even then busily engaged in buying quantities of furs from Canadian trappers. When they had consulted the minor details of the trip, without, however, mentioning at what point they crossed the border, much to Phil's disappointment, LeBlanc then told his companions that as soon as they had completed the deal in furs, that he had something very much bigger that would net them all a fortune. In fact, he told them, he would not have bothered with the fur trip at all, except that he and Anderson had used practically all their available money in buying furs.

From the bustling sounds of the room below, the others evidently crowded nearer to hear what this new scheme was, when suddenly there was a commotion at the door of the room below, and a voice was heard, demanding admittance.

"Ha," exclaimed Jean LeBlanc, "that is P'tit Vareau. I don't like him, and he shall not come in with us on this big scheme. Tomorrow night I shall discuss it with you at our friend M'sieu Henderson's place. Now, you may let him in, but not a word of anything other than about the furs."

Vareau made his entrance, and there was some desultory conversation, and then all of them left the room.

Phil's heart was bounding in excitement. Here he had all the details of the plot at his finger ends, and all that needed to be done was to keep close tabs on LeBlanc, and he would lead them direct to the headquarters of the smuggling crew.

Truly his attempt at escape next morning must not fail.

Garry and Dick, back at the lean-to, were discussing the possibility of Phil's stumbling upon important information, not knowing at that moment he was a prisoner, trapped in the old French restaurant, and in the hands of the most vengeful enemy that the three possessed.

Throughout the night they kept up a constant sentry duty, not that they really expected anything to happen, but just because it seemed to be better on the safe side—a case of rather be safe then be sorry. Morning came, and they prepared their breakfast. They did not dare to stir from the camp, for there was no telling at what moment they might get a message from Phil, telling them that their help was needed.

Despite the fact that he was worried, Phil slept the normal sleep of a healthy boy, awaking in the morning both hungry and thirsty. He immediately secured the iron tipped stick that he had fashioned the night before, and took his place at the door, ready to strike down whoever entered, and make a dash for liberty. Nearly two hours elapsed, and the strain was beginning to tell upon him, when he heard a sound of shuffling footsteps outside the door. Grasping his club firmly in his hand, he prepared to act, but to his keen disappointment, however, the door was opened only an inch or two, and he heard LeBlanc's voice, bidding him out. Through the crack of the door, he could see LeBlanc's form, and immediately in back of him, that of the big restaurant keeper.

He made no response for a moment, and suddenly the door was thrown open, and LeBlanc and the proprietor came rushing in. LeBlanc seemed to be possessed of second sight, for he seemed to know that Phil had contemplated an attack on whoever came in the room, and he foiled this by rushing at Phil, jamming him close to the wall, and making it impossible for him to raise his club, much less than to use it.

"Aha, mon brave would fight would he? I thought so, and came prepared to care for you. We will see that he has nothing left to fight with."

Bidding his companion in French remove the cot, LeBlanc cast a hasty glance around the room to see if anything was left that by any artifice whatsoever could be converted into a weapon. Phil had carelessly thrown the blanket over the hole that he had made on the floor, and in a fold had tucked away the piece of candle.

LeBlanc paid no attention to the blanket, seeming to think that with the cot broken the boy had slept on the floor. The table and the empty bottle that had served as a candlestick were removed, and then food and water was brought to him and left there.

"Tonight I am ver' busy, but tomorrow you shall be taken from here in a trunk, and you shall be dropped in the river. How you will like that, hein?" and with an evil grin he left the room, leaving Phil again in the darkness to eat his food as best he could.

Phil rescued his candle, and lighted it to eat by, and then carefully extinguished it, for he knew it would not last a great while were it to burn steadily.

He had one wild idea left. It was dangerous in the extreme, it might mean death, but it was death if he stayed in the clutches of the renegade half-breed. This idea was to try to set fire to the door, in the hopes that it would burn enough without setting the whole room on fire until he could battle his way out.

This idea he meant to carry out only as a last resort. There were two chances left to him. One was that he could find some other method of escape, the other was that his chums would come to his rescue when he failed to return at the appointed hour of sundown.

At any rate, he would wait until the last minute before trying his desperate scheme. LeBlanc, he knew, would be gone the greater part of the night, for they did not plan to start until almost midnight for Lafe Green's house.

The long day dragged on and he got hungry and thirsty. No one came again, evidently one meal was all that he was to have. Presently he decided that it must be past sundown, and he lay down on the blanket, and before he knew it dropped off to sleep.

Then out of a sound and dreamless sleep he heard a number of mysterious tappings on the iron shutter that guarded the window.

He ran to the window and listened again.

Yes, there they were, being repeated in a sort of a staccato yet rhythmic measure.

Suddenly it dawned on him what it was. The tappings were dots and dashes of the International Code, and they were spelling out:

P-H-I-L- P-H-I-L- P-H-I-L-

CHAPTER XIV.

CHUMS TO THE RESCUE.

To return now for a while to the lean-to we shall see what happened when sundown came and no Phil appeared.

"Oh, Dick, I'm sorry I let Phil go alone. We should have gone together, then there would have been less chance of anything having happened," said Garry brokenly.

"Cheer up, Garry, it's only a little past sundown, perhaps he didn't allow himself enough time to get back here, may have thought the distance was less than it was. You know he has been over this distance only two or three times. We'll give him a little while longer and then set our heads together and see what we can do. I have a lot of confidence in Phil, he manages to pull himself out of his scrapes pretty well most of the time," comforted Dick, although he too feared that Phil had gotten into some scrape that proved too much for him. Dick's fear was that Phil had run afoul of thetramps, for neither he nor Garry knew that LeBlanc was in that vicinity.

Nearly an hour passed, and then Garry sprang to his feet.

"There's no use waiting any longer. Phil would move heaven and earth to keep up to the agreement that was made as to the hour of return. Now we must do something. Get your rifle and lariat and hatchet. Stick the handle of the hatchet inside your trousers so that it will not be so evident, or better yet, we can do it just before we get to town. Then, too, we can coil our riatas over one shoulder, and slip our coats on over them. In that way we won't attract so much attention. The rifles won't appear to be out of place, for it would be only natural that we should take them, seeing we are supposed to be campers who will have to go back through the dark woods to camp. First, before we start, take our knapsacks, there's nothing in them that we will need, and cache them in the branches of a nearby tree. Then we'll leg it to town just as fast as we can."

Before Dick cached the knapsacks, Garry poured all the water in the canteens on the fire, thoroughly extinguishing it. Then in a trice the knapsacks were hidden in a tree, and the pair were ready to start for town.

Garry set a terrific pace at first, until Dick toned him down with:

"Look here, Garry, we don't want to get to town all tuckered out. If we do we will be useless if it comes to a pinch. I'm just as anxious about Phil as you are, but we must conserve our strength. We may need it before the night is over."

"Guess you're right old chap, but I just keep thinking that minutes may mean more right now than hours would some other time." Nevertheless he moderated his pace, and in a trifle under an hour they were in the town of Hobart.

Dick was for making at once to the restaurant to institute inquiries as to whether or not Phil had been there and when he was last seen. Garry by this time had grown calmer and cooler and again assumed the leadership.

"That would be a mighty foolish thing to do. If Phil has gotten into a scrape, there is just as good a chance that it was in that place as out in the street. You know we were warned that it wasn't a regular drawing room by any means. I have an idea, and I think you'll agree with me that it is a good one. We'll hike to the home of the chap we towed home with the broken arm the other day, and see if his granddaughter can give us a tip of any sort as to what sort of a place the restaurant is and what sort of a chap runs it and who hangs out there. Of course there is one great chance that Phil stumbled onto a real clue and followed it, but that is very remote, for I don't believe Phil would disobey an order that had been agreed upon by all as a safety measure."

"Jolly good idea, Garry," said Dick. "Let's go."

In a few moments they were at Mr. Everett's house, and were glad to find a light still burning there. They knocked on the door, and Ruth herself answered the knock.

"Goodness gracious," she exclaimed, in a surprised tone. "I never expected to see you boys at this time of night. Where's your other companion?"

"That's just what we would give anything in the world to know right now," remarked Garry. "We've come to you to see if you can give us a bit of help or information."

Then rapidly he told of the plans they had made to try and get evidence, and the agreement that Phil was to have returned at sundown that night.

"You say he went to the restaurant? Oh, that's a wicked place, and if he's gotten into trouble, that place is just where it would have been likely to happen. The owner of that place is dreadful. He helps those smugglers and sells contraband rum, and he and that half-breed LeBlanc have been suspected of several crimes along the border."

"What's that you say?" burst out Garry. "LeBlanc, you don't mean Jean LeBlanc?"

"Why, yes, do you know him or know of him?" returned the girl, amazed at Garry's sudden outburst.

"Yes, to our sorrow we do. I haven't time to tell you all we know of him now, except that he hates us like poison, since we were instrumental in having him jailed for kidnapping once, and then he broke out. Is that diabolic villain in town?"

"He is, I saw him only this afternoon. He used to be around here a great deal, for his original home is in a town not far on the other side of the border. I am so sorry to say it, but if your chum was in the restaurant and LeBlanc saw him there, he could have made him prisoner with the greatest of ease, for he has many friends there, and there are many who would do anything that rascally proprietor told them to."

"Does your grandfather know the ins and outs of that house?" inquired Garry.

"Yes, he does, but he is asleep, and as he had a bad day, the doctor says that he is not to be waked up under any circumstances, so I'm afraid you'll have to put up with my help, such as it is. All you have to do is wait till I run across the street and get Mr. Allen to come in and watch granddaddy and then I'll be ready to help you."

"You're a brick, Miss," said Garry enthusiastically, "but we couldn't think of letting you in for any danger."

"I guess you don't know the border girls, sir. We aren't afraid of anything in the woods or the towns. We've been brought up to take care of ourselves. Besides, I've heard Granddad tell about the Rookery, as he calls it, many times. An' I've an idea that if your chum is held a prisoner in that house, I know just where it is. So just you let me be your guide for a little while."

So saying, she ran across the street and soon returned with an elderly man, the Mr. Allen of whom she spoke, and then bidding the boys wait a minute, she dashed upstairs. In an incredibly short time she was back again, clad in a khaki skirt, high boots, and a heavy sweater. A knit tam was perched on her head, making her quite one of the most attractive girls the boys had ever seen.

"I'll lead you around to the back of the restaurant, where there won't be much chance of you're being observed. There's one window that has always puzzled me. It has a great heavy shutter on it, and I don't ever remember seeing it opened. I've always imagined it was the dungeon keep of the place, like the ones they used to have in old castles, long years ago."

Evidently, thought Garry, the young lady was of an extremely romantic turn of mind.

In a very few minutes she had led them through a dark back street to where they could command a view of the rear of the restaurant.

"There, wait till the moon comes out from behind that cloud. Now. See that window there all barricaded? That's what I think is the prison room for the Canuck's house," said Ruth.

The boys looked and saw the sinister window, which although they did not know it then, was the one to the room in which Phil was at that moment soundly sleeping, worn out by the mental and physical strain that he had been under for the past twenty-four hours.

Under the shuttered window ran a dark alleyway, and the other windows in that side of the house were dark and deserted looking. On the other side of the alley was a low blacksmith shop.

"Well, Garry, if you don't mind my calling you that, have you decided on what you are going to do?" asked Ruth. "I am afraid that you haven't much chance of getting upstairs if you go into the restaurant, for even if the proprietor is not there he has a couple of strong, ugly assistants, and if you tried to force your way upstairs at the point of a rifle, you would only bring the whole place down on you like a swarm of hornets. It's up to us to think out some scheme."

"I think I have that worked out now. See that chimney on the roof? It is just over that dark shuttered window. Now what I propose is this: Dick and I will get up on the roof of the blacksmith shop here, and from there we can throw a lariat up over the chimney, then one of us will go up hand over hand and call to Phil to see if he is in that room. If he is, we'll have him out as soon as you could say Jack Robinson. Miss Ruth, I'm going to ask you to stand guard for us, and if danger approaches, give us some sort of a signal. I suppose you can imitate a whippoorwill?" asked Garry.

"Indeed I can," and in a soft tone she proved it to the satisfaction of both Dick and Garry.

"There, then that much is accomplished. Believe me, I'll be overjoyed if I hear Phil's voice in answer to my hail," said Garry.

"Say, listen Garry. A fine business you'd make of calling through a thick shutter. First place maybe he couldn't hear it, but it's a cinch that everyone on the street will. Use your imagination. What did you ever learn wigwagging and signalling and things for? When you get to the window, take your knife and rap out a message in International Code. That will make no noise down here, but will penetrate into the room, for the shutter will form a natural sounding board."

"Fine, Dick. I must be wool gathering not to have thought of that myself. Now up on the roof with you."

Bracing himself against the wall, Garry formed a step for Dick to crawl up on the roof. Once arrived there, he lay flat, and extending his arms over the edge, gave a pull, and helped Garry up.

It took only four throws to settle the noose of the lariat over the chimney, and they let it swing down on the side of the building. Clambering down from the roof, Garry made ready to go up the rope. He went up in agile fashion, and soon was tapping on the shutter. It was his call that had awakened Phil.

When Phil heard it, he fished out his knife, and soon they were carrying on a brief conversation. Phil told Garry the inside of the shutter was sheathed with iron. Also he told him if anything happened to prevent them getting him out, to keep watch that night on Lafe Green's house, as there was a great plot on the way.

"I'll have you out in a jiffy now." Garry tapped the message to him, and then he slid down the rope. Dick and Ruth came running to him.

"Must have something to pry off that shutter with. My axe isn't strong enough," he told them.

"Oh, I know what," whispered Ruth. "I stumbled over something a minute ago, and it was a crowbar. Darius, the blacksmith, must have forgotten to take it in."

"Fine, let's have your riata, Dick. There, I'll loop it around my wrist and go back up the rope. In the meantime, you tie an end of it to the crowbar and I can haul it up to me."

So saying, Garry swarmed up the rope again. Arriving at the height of the window, he manoeuvered until he had twisted the free end of the rope around his foot several times, thus preventing himself from slipping.

Then he set to work to pry the shutter loose. Fortunately it did not long resist.

"Look out below," he warned softly, and with a loud thud the shutter fell into the alley below. Phil was waiting in the window.

"Quick, slide down after me. Lose no time, Phil," ordered Garry.

Down he went, the friction smarting his hands. In less time than it takes to tell, Phil was down after him. "Never mind the riata on the chimney. Away we go," said Garry.

"Follow me," ordered Ruth, and she sped away followed by the three chums. They were out of sight not a moment too soon, for as they turned acorner, running across a lawn to deaden their footsteps, they heard a howl of rage.

"That's the proprietor's assistant. We just got away in time," said Ruth.

CHAPTER XV.

THE PLOT.

Ruth led the boys to her home, explaining that it would be better for them to get out of sight as quickly as possible, lest they come upon one of their enemies.

"There's no danger of that just now," interrupted Phil, "for I know where most of them are at just this minute. However, it would be nice if you would take us to your home for a minute, for I think I have the keynote to the whole business right now, and I would like to tell my discoveries to Garry and Dick, and also get some directions from you, if you will sit in our council of war and act as chief advisor."

"Come right along. I must be getting back and let Mr. Allen go home. Also Granddad might have waked up, and we can get his advice," said Ruth.

Silently they followed her home. They heard no suspicious sounds, so evidently were not being followed. The chances were that the assistants of therestaurant keeper did not know what to do, and as Phil knew, none of the principals were about, and all that could be done was to await their return.

Garry hated to sacrifice his lariat, as it was an especially fine one, but there was no help for it, since getting it down would have led them all into certain capture again.

Arriving at the house, Ruth found that her grandfather was still asleep, while Mr. Allen was reading a magazine. He told Ruth that he would finish his story before going home, so that gave her an opportunity to hear Phil's story.

Hastily Phil went over the details of what had happened to him since leaving the boys the day before.

"Now the key to the entire matter seems to be the conference that is going to be held tonight at the home of this Lafe Green. He seems to be the leader of the entire business, but LeBlanc holds some sort of position of authority and will probably take the lead tonight, as he has some sort of a scheme to tell the others. They are planning a fur smuggling trip in the very near future, because Anderson is now in Canada buying skins for the trappers. Just what this new plan is I don't know, for just as he was going to tell it, a man called Vareau came to the room, and LeBlanc shut up like a clam, seeming not to like him."

"I wonder," said Garry reflectively, "if we couldn't get hold of this Vareau of whom you speak, and tell him his partners are leaving him out in the cold, and so get him to help us by leading us to the smuggling lane?"

"Don't have a thing to do with him," warned Ruth. "I don't blame LeBlanc for not wanting him to come in on any big plan, for he is like a snake and cannot be trusted even by those he is working for. Very likely if you tried to get his help, he would turn around and betray you to LeBlanc, hoping thereby to be taken in on the new plot."

"That's sound advice," said Garry. "On the whole, it is better for us to play a lone hand in this game, without taking anyone into our confidence, except you, Miss Ruth, for without you we might have failed tonight, and Phil lost forever."

"The first thing to do is to find Lafe Green's house and see if there is not some way in which we can get in to hear what they are planning. I know of no other way in which we can get the proper information, unless we appeal for help to the Customs authorities up the line, and have the entire outfit seized, but that would do us very little good, for we have no evidence on which to have them convicted, and besides that, we would lose all chance of stopping whatever big scheme is now in the wind. I suppose you can tell us where to find Green's house, can't you," asked Phil, turning to the girl.

"Yes, it is about a mile outside of the village in a lonely and secluded place. It is ostensibly a farm that he lives on, but I guess farming occupies but a small place in his mind. I only wish that I could go, and I believe I will see if I can't get Mr. Allen to stay here so I can guide you to the place," she answered, her eyes sparkling with the thought of the possible adventure.

But Garry firmly put his foot down on her running any chance of danger.

"In the first place, it would be bad enough if we were strangers to this crowd, for they would brook no interference with their plans, but there is the added danger in the fact that LeBlanc already has it in store for us, and anyone that takes side with us will meet with his vengeance and that of his friends. Besides, it is almost midnight," he said.

Reluctantly the girl gave up the idea of being in on the adventure.

"But what are your plans now?" she asked. "It seems that you are going on a wildgoose chase, just to go to Green's house, and besides, with all his friends there, you would have no chance of escape if your presence was discovered at the farm."

"Well, to tell the truth, all we can do is go there and be guided by circumstances. We cannot afford to let the slightest chance slip by us, and that seems just now to be the scene of plot, in fact it is the crux of the entire affair," responded Garry.

At that minute, however, fortune favored them. Mr. Allen came down stairs and told them that Mr. Everett was awake, and wanted the boys to come upstairs a minute and say hello to him.

After giving this message, he went home, and led by Ruth, the boys went upstairs to see Mr. Everett.

"Talk about luck!" whispered Garry to Dick. "Now we can get some real dope on all this."

Arriving at Mr. Everett's bedroom, they found him sitting up in bed with a heavy blanket thrown around his shoulders. He expressed his pleasure at seeing the boys again, and then inquired how it was that they happened to be around at such a late hour.

"Time is precious, so we'll have to give you an abbreviated account, sir," said Garry. "Phil, here, was captured by LeBlanc, one of our most vengeful enemies, and through the help of Miss Ruth here, we were able to rescue him," and Garry briefly told how they had broken open the window of the prison room, and released their chum.

"Now we have found out that something is going to take place at Lafe Green's house sometime after midnight, and it is imperative to our success thatwe go there immediately and see what can be done to find out what is being plotted. I am sure that we can put every trust in you, so I am going to confide in you. We are at present doing some work for the Customs authorities of the State, and as you are a former Customs agent, we are asking you for whatever aid you can give us," concluded Garry.

"H'm," said Everett. "Seems to me you are pretty young to be engaged in that kind of work. I suppose you have your credentials?"

"Indeed we have," and Garry drew from the cunningly made pocket in the waistband of his trousers the little gold shield that stamped them as members of the service.

"That is enough," said old Mr. Everett. "If it wasn't for my misfortune in being laid up, I would be with you tonight and between us we would have the goods on this outfit. As it is, you will have to take the chance yourselves, for I believe I can tell you just what to do. Some little time ago, I discovered a secret passage to Lafe Green's house. It is unlikely that anyone else in the village outside of myself and Green and his accomplices know about it. It wasn't built by Green, but by a former owner of the farm, who was in the same nefarious business. It may even be that Green does not know about it, although that is unlikely. This passage leads from the barn to the house, and was used to store contraband goods in. You see the stuff could be brought to the barn in a load of hay, or wood, and no one be the wiser. Then it could be hidden away in the secret passage, and a search party could look through the house and barn till doomsday and never discover it. Then, too, if the men were in danger of arrest, they could make their way to this passage, and after nightfall escape by way of the barn, as the authorities would of course have only the house under guard.

"This passage is entered by moving a feed box that stands at the end of the barn. When the box is moved away, you will see what appears to be nothing more nor less than ordinary flooring, but if you look carefully you will see a knot in one of the boards near the wall. Pry this out with your knife, and you will then be able to lift the cunningly contrived trap door.

This leads to the passage, which is more than forty feet long. The passage leads to the cellar of the house, entrance to the house being made by moving the trapdoor upwards. This requires a little effort, as it is covered by the dirt floor for three or four inches. In this trap is a ring to lift it when you want to get back to the passage. Once you have gotten through the trap, smooth the dirt back over it, leaving a chip or something directly over the spot where the ring is so you will waste no time in finding it when you want to go back.

"I must tell you this, however; once you get in the house, you will be in great peril, as these men are unscrupulous in the highest degree. Green would be behind the bars long before this except for good luck and the extreme precautions that he takes. Add to this the fact that many of the people in this section see no harm in smuggling, and would never give information even if they had it, and you can see how Green has so long managed to escape paying the penalty for his misdeeds. Now that is all I can tell you, and you had better be getting along on your work, as it is now midnight, and it will take you at least fifteen minutes to get to Green's barn."

Mr. Everett concluded by giving them minute instructions as to how to reach the farm of the suspected smuggler leader.

"I know all this is dangerous," said Mr. Everett, "but you boys are now working for your country, and as you have taken the responsibility you must be prepared to carry it out to the end. For safety's sake, however, I am going to propose the following measure. Come back to the house as soon as you have either succeeded or failed in your mission. If you are not here by six o'clock, I will take it on myself to summon help from the Customs authorities up the line, or arm a posse here and search Green's house. I hope that won't be necessary, for it would put an end to discovering what is in the wind, but that is better than that you boys should fall into trouble. Now God speed you on your way."

They said goodbye to Mr. Everett, after shaking hands with him, and once again hearing his wishes for good luck.

Ruth led the way to the door, shyly adding her own wishes for their success.

"Now you are sure you know the way?" she asked, as she opened the door. "I know I won't sleep a wink till you come back in the morning. Just ring the bell whenever you get back, and I will let you in. Good luck to you."

Walking at a brisk pace, they started for Green's farm. There was no moon, and it gave promise of rain, which suited the boys exactly, as there was now little chance of a stray shaft of light disclosing their presence when they arrived at their destination. At the end of fifteen minutes they reached the farm, and carefully making their way across the field, came to the barn, standing like a great black hulk. The boys thrilled with excitement, for they felt they were on the last lap in the search for the smuggler band, that it was their mission to put an end to.

CHAPTER XVI.

DANGEROUS BUSINESS.

"Now fellows," whispered Garry, "duck around the side of the barn here, while I tell you what I doped out as we walked along. Keep an eye out for dogs."

They followed Garry's lead around the barn.

"Here's what I doped out. Only one of us can enter the house. To have more do it might spell disaster to our plans, for in case of danger one could find a hiding place where two could not. Two of us will go into the barn, while one stays out here as guard. Once in the barn, the feed box will be moved, and the one to enter the passage will do so, while the other replaces the feed box, and rejoins the man on guard. It is now twelve-thirty, and the man who enters the house ought to hear all that's going on and be able to make a getaway in at least three hours and a half, probably a lot sooner. That is allowing the men an hour or more for talking, as they probably will take no longer, and two hours or two hours and a half for everything to get quiet and allow the man in the house to get away. Now to settle who goes into the house, we will follow our custom of drawing lots. Phil is out, for he has already been in danger once, and furthermore, he has had his share of adventure. That leaves it up to either Dick or I to go in. Phil, get your knife out and hold it in one of your hands. Then Dick and I will each choose a hand and the one who guesses rightly will enter the passage."

Phil did as he was bade, and then Garry told Dick to take first choice of hands.

"Right hand," said Dick, after a pause.

"Garry goes," whispered Phil. "I had my knife in my left hand."

Dick muttered a muffled exclamation of disappointment, for he had counted on being the one to undertake the dangerous mission, but he abided by the lot.

Leaving Phil on guard outside the door, Garry and Dick noiselessly rolled back one of the folding doors just enough to allow them to slip through.

The inside of the barn was as black as a pocket. Standing there for a minute or two, the boys waited in silence. They could hear the uneasy stamping of a horse, awakened probably by their entrance.

After what they judged to be a safe interval, Garry snapped on his flashlight, and threw the beam of light playing about the floor, keeping it on only long enough to get a general impression of the interior, and being careful not to allow its rays to strike upward lest it be seen through a window.

What they saw made it apparent that Mr. Everett's words about farming playing a small part in Green's life proved true. There was a single horse in the barn, and one good wagon. The farming implements appeared to be suffering from long disuse.

Garry located at the end of the barn the feed box that marked the passage entrance.

Hastening to it, they moved it forward, and there, as told them by Ruth's grandfather, was the knot. Getting his knife out, Garry dug at the knot which yielded to his efforts and came out.

The trap was lifted, and Garry, shaking hands with Dick, made ready to enter. A musty odor emanated from the passage, making it evident that it had not been used for a long time.

"Push the box back over the passage when I get in," he whispered to Dick. "When I come to get out, I can tip it over when I push upward on the trap. Now you hustle back out and rejoin Phil. Wait for me down the road under that big elm tree that we passed on our way here. I noticed that there was a field back of it, and in case you hear anyone coming along, you can slip back into it and hide until he or they have passed on. Now see you later," and snapping on his flashlight, went down the crude ladder that gave entrance to the passageway.

He waited at the bottom of this ladder until he heard the crunching sound of the feed box being pushed back over the trap door. Then the light of the flashlamp ahead of him in a dancing beam, his heart beating rapidly with excitement, he pushed on.

He was almost startled into an exclamation of dismay, as there came the sound of a squeal, and a small form scurried across his feet. Then he laughed with relief, for it was nothing more than a small rat.

After walking what he judged to be about twenty feet through the passage, which was shored up and roofed with timbers much after the manner of a mine tunnel, he approached a spot where the passage widened, and he found he was in a sort of room.

At one side were a number of casks, but these were empty, as Garry found when he stirred one of them with his feet. At the other side of the room was a crude table, built of pine boards. On this table reposed a stack of fine fur, roped into a bundle. Garry examined it and found the skins to be those of fine seals, caught in Canadian waters, and destined to be sent to New York and sold to some woman who would have no idea that the law of the land had been broken by the making of the coat or neckpiece that she would be wearing.

They had been there for some time, Garry judged, for the dust was thick enough to denote that no one had been there for some days.

He pushed his way on through the passage, and came at last to the end. There was a box to stand on so that one might get up high enough to get a good purchase on the trap.

Now came a crucial moment. There was no telling whether or not the cellar was occupied. All that Garry could do was to push upward and trust to chance. Very carefully and slowly he pushed upward.

It required some exertion, but finally gave way. Pushing it three or four inches, Garry paused, and both looked and listened. There was not a sound, and no beam of light came to disclose the presence of anyone in the cellar.

Giving the trap a last upward fling, Garry was soon in the cellar. Pressing the snap of his light so that it would continue to shine, he covered the trap with the dirt, smoothing it with his hands so that it would show no signs of having been recently displaced.

The first step had been successfully negotiated. Now remained the difficult task of getting upstairs and in a place where he could hear what was being plotted by Green, LeBlanc and their friends.

Walking as near the edge of the steps as he could, for it is at this point that they are less apt to creak, he made his way up the cellar stairs.

Every step was now one of potential danger, for the throwing open of the kitchen door would disclose his presence, and he would be trapped, for there was no exit from the cellar except through the passageway, and he knew that if he were discovered, some of the men would run to the barn and guard that exit. His rifle had been left with the boys, for it would only be a hindrance in his movements in getting into the house.

After a few moments he reached the top of the stairs, and with his ear pressed to the door, listened for sounds that would tell him whether or not the kitchen was occupied. He heard nothing, and then bent to where the latch pierced the door. He could see no bit of light shining through the small crevice, and then carefully raised the latch, taking nearly a minute to do so, that it might give no sharp, warning click.

The latch once raised, he pushed the door open carefully, shoving it barely a fraction of an inch at a time.

After what seemed almost ages, Garry stepped into the kitchen. He knew it was dangerous to press the button on his flashlamp, but there was nothing else to be done, for he could not go moving through the dark, taking the chance of crashing into a chair or table, and thus advertising his presence in the house.

Throwing the beam of light sweeping along the floor for an instant, and concentrating with all his might, he impressed on his mind a mental picture of the interior of the room, noting two doors and locating the various pieces of furniture in the kitchen.

His next act was to untie hastily the strings of his shoepacks, and slipping out the footgear, knotted the laces and strung the shoepacks about his neck. He was now able to move noiselessly.

Standing silently, he listened. He could hear the murmur of voices beyond one of the doors. His heart leaped, for there were probably the plotters. He crept to the door, and listened, but could make out nothing of what was being said. Only an indistinct murmur reached his ears.

It would be foolhardy to try and open the door, for he could not hope to do it without letting those in the room know it, even with all the luck in the world.

Garry was stumped. He began to wish that he had taken a chance and approached the house from the outside, trusting to fortune to get to a window through which he might both see and hear.

The boy stood for a moment and debated as to what was the best course to pursue, whether to go back through the passage and try and approach from the outside, or what.

Then he recollected the other door. Knowing that the construction of old New England houses generally called for a front and back stairs, he guessed that this other door would lead to the upper part of the house.

Noiselessly crossing the floor, he cautiously opened the door, and found that his guess was right, for a single flash of his lamp showed a flight of stairs.

His stockinged feet making no sound, he crept up the stairs. At the top of the flight was another door, and opening this a bit at a time, he entered the room. All was darkness and silence.

He swept his flashlamp around the room, and made a discovery that promised the means of hearing what was going on in the room the plotters were in.

In most small towns, and especially in farm houses, a furnace is an unknown quantity. So to provide heat for the upper rooms without going to the expense of getting extra stoves, holes about a foot in diameter are cut through the ceiling, and an iron grating called a "register" is installed. This allows the heat to mount to the upper rooms.

Garry mentally estimated the location of the room he was in, and decided that it was over the kitchen. Hence the next room on that floor must be the one over that in which the conference of the smugglers was taking place.

Walking as though the floor were covered with eggs, he proceeded to the other door of the room, and pursuing the same tactics of taking several moments, cautiously opened the door. He found that he was in a bedroom. He stood stock still, and listened.

The room was unoccupied, for there was no sound of breathing coming from the direction of the bed. Deciding to get his bearings before going further, he looked about. By this time his eyes had become accustomed to the dark, and he did not make use of his lamp. A faint bit of light proved to be coming through the window. Creeping across the floor, he examined. It was open, for the night was warm.

Outside the window was a great maple tree. One branch was almost on a level with the sill and not more than two feet distant.

This done, he searched for the light that would disclose the location of the register, and his heart fell when he found nothing. It seemed as if his carefully planned move had fallen like a house of cards.

Since there was evidently no register in the room, it seemed safe to flash his lamp.

It must be explained that Garry's examination of the room occupied only a matter of seconds.

Just as he was about to press the button of the flashlight, he heard the purring voice of LeBlanc, muffled and indistinct.

With a thrill of excitement, he knew that there was a register in the room after all. Getting down on his hands and knees, he felt about the floor. Only the bare boards were his reward, until as he approached the bed he felt a heavy rag rug.

Feeling over this, he discovered it to be slightly raised in the middle. Carefully rolling it back, he was rewarded by seeing light and hearing the hum of voices.

At last Garry was an unseen listener to the plot being hatched below!

CHAPTER XVII.

THE RUSSIAN'S TALE.

Garry crawled under the bed, laying so that he could both look down into the room and hear what was being said. Then he arranged the rug that it could be flipped back into place in an instant.

Then he peered down into the room below. One was Jean LeBlanc, who, of course, he knew. The second man he placed as Lafe Green, a great hulk of a man with flaming red hair. He recognized him from the description given by Ruth. The other three were strangers. Two wore the ordinary garb of the woods, but the third was dressed in well-made clothes. He was a striking looking man with a lustrous black beard and moustache.

As Garry listened, LeBlanc again took up the conversation. It seemed that the details of the trip to bring the consignment of furs across the border had been settled. Garry was sorry he was too late to hear this, but of course there was no help.

"Now we shall come to the main business of the evening, ma fren's. I have already told you, this man, his name is Boris Borefski, who comes from Russia with a great scheme, a fine scheme, oui, it is magnifique. Beside it, the bringing of a few furs is nothing. Were it not for the fact the furs have been bought, pouf! we should throw away the plan like so many dead leaves. M'sieu Boris shall himself tell you his story. He speaks not the English, so me, I shall act as the interpreter and tell you what he says as he goes along. Eh bien, M'sieu, begin."

Speaking rapidly in French, as many well educated Russians are able to do, and being stopped occasionally by LeBlanc while a translation was being made, Boris began:

"My new acquaintance and already my good friend LeBlanc has told you that I have a plan. True I have, one that will make for us all much money.

"I was for many years the private secretary to the Grand Duke Sidis in Russia, a man immensely wealthy. Among his prized possessions were a number of magnificent jewels. They were only second in value to those of the Grand Duke Boris, cousin to the Czar.

"Of course you know what happened during the war, how the masses arose against the Czar and took the government away from the ruling classes. At first all went well, and then the Bolshevists began their reign. When the homes of the wealthy were raided and despoiled of their valuables, my master confided in me, and together we contrived a secure hiding place for the jewels.

"To save my own life, I pretended to be one of the Bolshevists. But, bah, they were nothing to me. All the time I thought and thought of the magnificent jewels hidden away from the light of day where the Grand Duke and I had placed them.

"The more I thought, the more I pondered over why I should stay in that land, or why I should continue to live a life of poverty. Confiding in my brother, who had joined the Bolshevists as I had, merely to protect his life, we decided that we should make a break for liberty, taking with us the jewels of the Duke.

"Scraping together all the money we could by any means whatsoever, we took the gems one night and fled. Of the long trip across Siberia I shall not bother to tell you; it is sufficient to say that we suffered much. Finally we reached the end, and in a big Japanese fishing vessel were brought to the western part of Canada.

"In British Columbia we made an attempt to cross the border, but in some way suspicion rested upon us, and again we fled. A Canadian Customs man followed us all the way across Canada, but we managed to give him the slip and we landed in the home town of my good friend LeBlanc. Fortune favored us, for we made his acquaintance.

"He has agreed that he will help us bring the jewels across the border, and more than that, he will help us sell them in places he and his companion Green know about. For all of you there is much pay if you help. And that is all there is to tell you," concluded the Russian.

Without waiting for any reply, the Russian fished in an inside pocket, and brought out a small leather bag.

"See, here is only one small part of the fortune," and as he spoke he unloosed the string and shook out on the table a magnificent bracelet, set with diamonds.

In the light of the oil lamp that stood on the table, it flashed and sparkled. The men gazed admiringly at it, and Garry himself could scarcely restrain a gasp of astonishment.

LeBlanc silenced the talk of the men and said:

"We shall help this man in his work, for the pay will be great, very great. The plans to be made are simple. Tomorrow night we shall bring the furs over the regular route and store them in Green's place here till our friends with whom we deal come after them. Saturday night when all is quiet we shall bring the jewels here, where our friend will give us as pay a share of the jewels."

Turning to the Russian he explained something that Garry had wanted to hear since he and his chums had started on their mission; this was the location of the lane over which the stuff was brought.

"We cross the border at a point almost on a line with Green's house here, for then we can come down through the woods and across the fields with little danger of being seen by anyone. Once we are here we are safe, for Lafe here has a place to hide things that is beyond discovery."

Although pressed to stay for a while and join a card game that was about to start, he refused, declaring that he was tired and needed sleep, and would return to the place he was staying for the night, meaning, Garry decided for himself, the restaurant and rooming house conducted by LeBlanc's French friend.

Lafe let the Russian out and then returned to the room, rubbing his hands together with the thought of the big reward they would get for their help in the smuggling of the jewels across the border.

As he returned, one of the men asked:

"I say, Jean, what pay will we get for all this business?"

104

"Ah, ma fren's, we will get big pay, trust Jean to see to that. Did I not tell you tonight I had the big plan in my head? You have not heard the whole of that plan. Once we get those jewels across the border, we shall simply help ourselves to the whole of them. That will be our pay, share and share alike."

The others looked at Jean in amazement, for this thought had never entered their heads.

"What about old Whiskers, the Russian, and his brother?" asked one.

"Pouf, what can they do? They can appeal to no one, for they are trying to break the law and would only get prison for their pains. We have only to laugh at them. Now let us have a little game of cards, while Lafe goes to the cellar for some of that very excellent stuff he has in there."

Garry thanked fortune that he had not obeyed an impulse to hasten to the cellar and make his getaway while the Russian was being let out.

Then he was startled almost out of a year's growth at the turn that events took at that moment.

"You fellows can play cards all you want, but go out in the kitchen. There's a big table there," said Lafe.

That meant to Garry that his retreat was to be cut off as long as the card game was in progress. This might be so long as to exceed the time limit set for his return to Dick and Phil, and consequently give them cause to worry.

Then followed disaster number two.

"If you chaps want to play cards and drink, you can do it without me. I'm dog tired, too tired even to go home, and I'm going upstairs and turn in for a while," said one of the quartet.

"All right, if you want to, take the room over this one," said Green.

Escape seemed to be cut off at all angles from Garry, not to mention the chances of detection.

Quickly flipping the rug back in place over the register, he rolled back under the bed, hugging up against the wall as close as he could. He didn't know what he was going to do. For the present the only thing possible was to remain where he was, trusting to chance not to be detected.

For a moment he thought of making a dash for the hall or the other room, but decided the danger was too great. It was well that he remained where he was, for the door opened, and the man came in, yawning audibly.

He threw his clothes off and tumbled into bed, while Garry hardly dared breathe for fear that his presence would be detected.

Fortunately the man was so tired that he did not lay awake long, and his stentorous breathing soon told Garry he was asleep. Garry took counsel with himself as to what was the best course to follow. He could stay where he was till the card game broke up, and then steal down the stairs and backthrough the cellar passageway, or he could make his way down the front stairs and try and let himself out of the front door. There was one drawback to this. Green might have locked the front door and pocketed the key, and then, too, there was the danger that one of those remaining up might go wandering through the house just as Garry made the attempt.

There was one other alternative. He could remain in the house till morning, and then when they had all gone, make his way out easily. Then Garry remembered that this was impossible, as Everett would have a posse come to the house if he were not back at six. That would be disastrous now, for it would halt the bringing of the jewels across the border, and Garry was determined that their seizure should be part of the grand finale in cleaning up the smuggler gang.

He must get out of the house as soon as possible. But how?

Then he bethought himself of the tree outside of the window. He remembered that the branch swung very close to the house. Could he make his way out of the window, then he could swing onto the branch, and so descend to the ground with no danger of being discovered.

The only element of danger was that the man should wake as he was making his escape. Still Garry reflected, he had been in a tight place ever since the moment he had entered the passageway, and this would be no worse.

Assuring himself that the man was still sleeping soundly, he began to edge his way from under the bed. His way across the floor was one of infinite precaution, taking many minutes. After he had squirmed for a foot or so, he would stop and listen to see if the regular breathing of the man on the bed continued. Once as he was half way across the floor, he heard a creak, as the sleeper rolled over in his slumbers.

Garry didn't dare to move for nearly five minutes after this. Then he started again, and after what seemed an age, reached the window.

Cautiously he raised himself up, and thrust a leg out of the window. Then followed the other, and he was sitting on the sill. Leaning out, he let his body fall towards the limb, caught it, and swung clear of the window.

In a trice he had thrown his leg up over the tree, his practice in the gymnasium making this an easy feat. Crawling carefully along the limb, he worked his way to the trunk, and then the descent to the ground was accomplished without trouble. Without bothering to put on his shoepacks, he sped away from the house.

Finally he reached the road, and here he slipped the heavy shoepacks on, and in a few moments had rejoined his companions where they were nervously waiting under the big elm.

They hailed his coming with delight, pounding him on the back and shaking hands gleefully.

"What luck, old topper?" was Dick's first question.

"All the luck in the world, boys. Tonight our quest was crowned with success!"

CHAPTER XVIII.

FERNALD COMES.

"Tell us all about it," demanded Phil.

"All in good time," responded Garry. "First thing to do now is to put a bit of distance between us and that house. Don't want any of that gang to come and find us snooping around. Everything has gone as slick as a whistle so far, and we don't want any foolish oversight to queer it. I move we make a break for town and hive in somewhere and wait for daylight. Of course we can go to Everett's house, but we shouldn't bust in on him in the middle of the night. He's a sick man, you know."

"Wonder where we can go and talk things over," asked Dick. "I suppose we could go and duck in the woods a ways and build a bit of a fire, for it seems a bit chilly."

"There's one place we can go and never be bothered. That's down to the station. It never opens till six o'clock. I inquired of the agent when we arrived; didn't know but what the information might come in useful some time. Besides, there's a bench in front where we can sit and gas away without anyone hearing us. Then just before six we can hike to Everett's house, so that he won't be raising a rescue party."

All this conversation took place as the boys were walking. In a short time they had arrived at the station. The fitful gleam of an oil lamp on a bracket over the bench was the only light, although in a short time, now, the first light of early dawn would begin to break.

The weary boys threw themselves on the bench, while Garry proceeded to give an account of his night's venture. The chums listened with breathless interest as he told of the developments, and held their breath as Garry told of the dangerous business of getting out of the room with the man there on the bed.

"Gosh," said Dick, "I'd have given a good bit to be in on that. Strikes me that you and Phil have had all the fun out of this proposition."

"Sure we've had some fun out of it, but it's only evening things up a bit. Remember that it was you who had the honor of finding the hermit that time we were in search of him, and Phil had to stay behind without getting a chance, although he got into a pickle afterward," said Garry consolingly.

"Guess we can't have everything in this world," answered Dick. "Next thing to do now is to plan our new campaign. Of course we won't bother with them tomorrow night, for that is small potatoes compared to the jewel plot. Isn't that LeBlanc a cold blooded specimen of a human being? He'd double cross his own father. I doubt if he would have the slightest hesitation about putting the Russians out of the way if he couldn't achieve his ends in any other way."

"Dare say you're right, Dick. At any rate, we must now put our heads together and dope out just what to do in this smuggling case. What must be done is to capture them just as they get over the border. Then the gems will be found in their possession, and they will be caught dead to rights. If they are allowed to reach Green's house, there are any number of ways they can squirm out of the mess provided they have a clever lawyer. I don't know but what the best plan is to tell this whole business to Mr. Everett and see what he suggests. I imagine that his advice will be to get help from the Customs house up the line, and then lay in wait for them. There'll probably be a hot time taking them, so you'll come in for a share of the excitement after all, Dick."

This having been settled, there was nothing more to do except to chat away the time till morning. As they talked, the first faint flush of dawn appeared in the east, giving promise of a fine day despite the fact that the moonless night had hinted of rain.

Finally Garry looked at his watch.

"Just five o'clock," he announced. "In another few minutes we start for the Everett home. By the way, that Miss Ruth is a brick."

He said it so enthusiastically that Dick and Phil looked at each other and then burst into a shout of laughter. Both saw a chance to have a little fun at the expense of their leader.

"What do you know about that, Phil," said Dick, giving Phil a nudge as he spoke. "I believe upon my soul that Garry has been smitten with the charms of the fair lady."

"Looks very much that way," responded Phil, falling into the spirit of the joke.

Garry turned a dark red.

"Of all the confounded foolishness, that is the worst," he sputtered. "Why, I've only seen the girl a couple of times."

"Methinks thou dost protest too much," quoted Dick.

"And as for me, I'll have something to tell a certain young lady back home," announced Phil.

Garry again broke into indignant denials.

"By George, Phil, I only said that in joke, but now I think that I hit the nail on the head," declared Dick. As a matter of fact, both he and Phil were now sure that their joke was more flavored with truth than jest.

Just as they were preparing to leave, they heard a distant rumble.

"There's a train headed this way. Wonder if it's a freight or a passenger," remarked Phil.

"Must be a freight, there are no passengers scheduled to pass here at this time of day," said Garry. "Shall we wait and watch it go by? That seems to be the only thing in the way of excitement that is promised for this morning."

The others being agreeable, they waited a moment. Soon the puffing engine appeared at the curve, and the rumbling grinding cars passed them. The boys amused themselves by checking off the various railroad lines that were represented by the markings on the different freight cars. They noted the Grand Trunk and Canadian Pacific predominated, giving rise to the thought that this was bound for the far west via the Canadian Rockies.

As the caboose appeared in sight, the train seemed to slacken speed for a bit, and a man jumped off the back end, waving a goodbye to the train crew as he did.

"Well, talk about luck," shouted Garry, as he saw the features of the man. "There's Fernald, the Customs agent!"

He was right, and as soon as Fernald saw them, he hailed them, asking in surprise how they knew he was going to arrive at that time, and on a freight instead of a passenger train.

"To tell you the truth, Mr. Fernald," explained Garry, "you were the last man on earth that we expected to see right this minute. The reason for our being here involves the telling of a long story, and we must keep a six o'clock engagement in order to prevent an armed posse from going in search of us. Perhaps you'd better come along, and then we can tell you the story at the same time we tell Mr. Everett."

"Who's Everett?" asked Fernald quickly.

"Oh, he's a fine old chap, used to be collector at the Customs House when it was located here some years ago. We did him a slight favor a little while ago, and he repaid us very handsomely by giving us information that was the means of our getting a clue that means the capture of the gang Sunday night," answered Garry, as they walked along.

They reached the Everett house just on the stroke of six, and were admitted by Ruth even before they rang the bell. Evidently she had been watching for them from the window.

"Oh, I'm glad you are back all safe and sound. I worried so that I hardly slept, and Granddad woke me three or four times to know if you had comeback. His orders were to have you go right up the minute you came. But who is this gentleman?"

"Pardon me, Miss Ruth, this is Mr. Fernald, one of the men of the service, and he will take charge from now on. We're thankful he came, for we were almost up a stump as to how to proceed now," said Garry. Indeed all three were thankful that Fernald had arrived, for they felt the need for the counsel of an older head than theirs, and one more experienced in the work of capturing a smuggler outfit than were they.

They found Mr. Everett in the act of struggling to tie a tie with one hand, and muttering fiery exclamations at his failure to accomplish the feat speedily. Garry did the job for him, and after Fernald had been introduced, they went over the story again.

Just before he started, old Mr. Everett, looking searchingly at Fernald, said:

"I remember you now. You were connected with that Harworth smuggling case nearly eighteen years ago. I was one of the witnesses then."

"Why, I remember you too, now," said Fernald, his face lighting up. At first he had been a little dubious about the boys having confided so much of their business to a stranger, but this new development cleared away all doubt.

Garry told the whole story of the night's happenings, amazing his hearers with the tale of his pluck and good fortune.

After the telling of the story, Ruth hastened away to prepare breakfast for all, insisting that they stay, although they protested against causing so much trouble.

"Oh, it won't be a bit of trouble. It will be fun, because it isn't often that I cook for anyone but Granddad and myself. Besides, I'll probably make Garry help me wipe the dishes." With that she darted from the room.

Phil and Dick burst into a shout of laughter.

"Aha, it seems that the same arrow has hit two people," Dick whispered to Phil, but loud enough so that Garry could hear. He blushed furiously, but could be drawn to make no comment or denial.

"Now the next thing on the docket is to discover the exact trail taken by these men on their smuggling trip. We know it will be the same on both nights, but of course we won't molest them on the first trip. This big gem plot overshadows all others. The question is, just how to find that trail."

"If you will allow me to make a suggestion, I think I can solve that problem after I ask a question or two of Mr. Everett," interposed Garry.

112

"Go to it, you boys have done the trick so far, now go on and finish it," said Fernald heartily.

"First, then," said Garry, "how far is the boundary line at a point just back of Green's farm, and how dense is the woodland there, Mr. Everett?"

"Why, as the crow flies, it is about three miles, maybe a little less. And as for the woodage, it is quite sparse. You see the logging operations extended that way, and they very nearly clean cut that land. There are, however, a few big trees scattered here and there. On the other side of the border, the forest gets considerable thicker."

"Fine, I see a way very clearly now," said Garry. "Sometime today, LeBlanc and Green, with the other two men, whose names I do not know, will cross the border, for they are due to return tonight with furs. Dick, Phil and I will estimate as near as we can the point on the line at the back of Green's farm. Then we will take positions about a sixteenth of a mile apart, perhaps a little more. We can mount one of the taller trees, and with our glasses can keep a sharp lookout for the point where they cross the line. It is likely that from force of habit they will take the same route going as returning. That will allow us to cover a quarter of a mile, counting in what we can see without glasses on either side. Then on Saturday we can repeat the operation, if necessary, thus getting a double check on the route. We know how to get our bearings and mark the trail so that we can find it again, even in the dark."

"That's the ticket. That will be your work for today then, while I go up the line and arrange for a posse of Customs men and deputies to effect the capture of Sunday night," said Fernald.

They could detect the welcome smell of boiling coffee and bacon and eggs, and at that moment Ruth called them to breakfast.

CHAPTER XIX.

SMUGGLERS' LANE.

"Shall we give you a lift downstairs, Mr. Everett?" asked Garry.

"Say, do you fellows take me for a confounded child?" snorted Mr. Everett. "Just because I get bruised up a little is no sign that I'm a helpless invalid. I'll go downstairs by the help of myself and no one else."

"What's that I hear, Granddad?" demanded Ruth, from the bottom of the stairs. "You are not to stir a single step unless you let two of the boys help you."

"There, dang it, Ruthie, can't you let me save my pride in front of these youngsters? All right, all right, have it your own way. But I warn you, one of these days you'll boss me too much, and then well see, we'll see."

As the boys, a little embarrassed by the turn of events, were helping him down the stairs, he whispered delightedly:

"Bosses me round just like a youngster, that girl does. Only way I can save my pride is to let on that I'm awful put out about it. But Lord bless you, if she didn't boss me, I wouldn't know what to do," he concluded with another chuckle of pleasure.

The boys then perceived that Ruth's "bossing" was evidently a daily occurrence, a sort of family joke, and joined in laughing with old Mr. Everett, who seemed to take such keen delight in "saving his pride."

Breakfast was a jolly affair. The eggs were done to a turn, the bacon crisp, the coffee like drops of amber, and the hot biscuits would fairly melt in one's mouth. They chatted merrily while they ate. Suddenly it occurred to Garry to ask how it was Fernald had arrived that morning.

"Why I got the whole dope on the receiving end of the fur smuggling by your tip on the two buyers, and have that ready to clean up any time I want to. Then I got worrying about you boys here in a strange country, and decided to hop on and lend what assistance I could. I got as far as I could by passenger train, and then because of bad connections, got waylaid and found I would have had to lay over. Fortunately that fast freight came along, and by dint of a little persuasion managed to convince the trainmen that I was not a tramp, but on government business, with the result that I arrived here fourteen hours quicker than I would have otherwise. It was a piece of good fortune, for I guess I am here in just enough time to see the finish of a thrilling case, minus the thrills for me."

Breakfast over, Fernald said he was off for the Customs House, while the boys prepared for a long vigil at the border to spot the "lane" used by the smugglers in their trips.

Ruth insisted on preparing a lunch for them, and packed it so it could be comfortably slipped in the pockets, so that no excess baggage would bother them.

Before starting out, Garry climbed to the attic of the Everett house, and getting the range with his glasses, computed the distance by means of the Mill scale on the glasses. This gave him a working plan to use when they hit the border, and could direct their steps so as to come out almost exactly back of the Green farm. All that they needed to know was the distance from the Everett House to the border. Ruth informed them it was a matter of almost exactly three miles and a half, so they were now sure of their distances and course. By making straight north for the border, they would have the advantage of avoiding going through the main part of the town.

Starting out, the three made their way directly to the approximate location of the border line. They kept track of the distance by using a careful thirty inch step, such as is used in the regular army, and counting their paces as they went. A pace consists of two steps, and is measured by starting off with the right foot and counting every time the left foot strikes the ground. This makes each pace just five feet, and as there are five thousand, two hundred eighty feet in a mile, one can estimate when he has paced a mile within a very few feet.

Arriving at the general point where the imaginary line ran, they branched off at right angles and walked the necessary distance to bring them to a location in line with the Green farm. To make sure, Garry climbed to the top of a tree, and with his glasses soon spotted the farm.

Garry elected to stay at this point, and instructed his companions to pace a sixteenth of a mile to either side, and there find a likely tree and mount it to keep their long vigil.

"We ought not to have to wait a great length of time, for they will have to get to their destination to get the furs and come back again, since they intend to bring them tonight," said Garry. "There doesn't seem to be any way that we can signal to each other in the event that they see the men pass, so I suggest that a full half hour wait be made after the man or men, for they will probably all go together, or at very near intervals, have passed and then duck back to this tree where I am holding out, and report. We all know what LeBlanc and Green look like, but Dick here never saw the other two accomplices, so I'll describe them carefully. Wait until they have all crossed before leaving your post, and when you do, be on your guard every step of the way, to prevent surprise."

Garry then described the men for Dick's benefit, and assuring himself that all instructions were understood, dispatched the chums to their posts, and then selected the tree that he intended to use for a post. Climbing up into the branches so that he would be out of sight, and yet be able to command a view, he made himself as comfortable as possible, although there was no rocking chair ease. Taking off his coat he made a sort of a cushion of it, in the crotch formed by the juncture of two heavy branches and made ready for his wait.

Nearly two hours passed without his seeing a sign of any approach, and the uncomfortable seat began to be irksome. Occasionally he stretched himself by climbing up into the tree a ways, and then back again.

He was beginning to think that he had bargained for too much, to guarantee to stay there and watch for the approach of the smugglers.

Another hour passed, and he began to be stiff and strained. At that moment he heard a whistle, a succession of different notes which he at once recognized as a signal often used by the three when they were approaching each other.

In a few moments Dick loomed into view.

Garry, rescuing his coat and rifle, slid down the tree and hailed him with the all important question as to whether he had found what they came in search of.

"Bet you I did," promptly responded Dick, when the question had been put. "They came in a clump almost. First the two chaps you described, and about five minutes after, LeBlanc and Green breezed by, not letting any grass grow under their feet. I've marked the spot well, and have located a good trail all the way, using private signs of our own that would be meaningless even to a woodsman familiar with all trail markings and signs. Fact I discovered one or two unfamiliar trail signs, that I could not recognize, and I believe they are the ones put there by a smuggler band. I'm pretty certain that is the regular trail used. Are you stiff? Believe me, that is the last tree sentry duty I want for a long time to come. I'd as soon sit two hours on a telegraph wire as the limb of a tree. Let's hike after Phil and return to town. Guess we've done all that we can."

"Yes, nothing remains now to be done except wait for the big doings Saturday night. Let's go, and keep a sharp lookout all the time. By the way, how near did they pass to you?"

"Not more than twenty feet above where I was located. Evidently they do not cut a straight line from the farm, but slant a little, unless our reckoning was a bit off. It is likely that they swerve a bit, because there may be a pathway across the farm that they use to get here. Believe me, I held my breath as they went by, although there was little danger of their seeing me. I strained my ears to see what they might be talking about, but could get nothing, as they talked in a low tone," answered Dick.

In a few minutes they had come to where Phil was perched, and he clambered down and met them. They told him the latest developments, and then struck out for town.

"I'm all in for a little sleep. I move we go back to Everetts', and ask them to loan us a couch or a bed or something for a couple of hours or so. I believe I could sleep for a year."

"That's a good idea. Mr. Everett said that we were to consider the house as headquarters until the game was bagged, so there would be no danger of our running into a scrape and spoiling the plans," remarked Garry.

The thought of a nap made them hasten their steps, and soon they were back at the house. Ruth admitted them, and after telling her and her grandfather of their success, proposed a nap.

"You deserve it, certainly. You can use the big double room, there are two beds in it, and turn in till suppertime. Fernald won't be back before then, and there's nothing to keep you up," said Mr. Everett.

The tired boys soon tumbled into bed, and without any preamble, dropped off to sleep. They had slept what seemed to them to be only a few minutes, when they were awakened by Fernald.

"Tumble up now, it's six o'clock, and the young lady downstairs says that supper will get cold if you wait any longer."

A liberal application of cold water soon aroused them, and in a little while they were doing justice to the ample meal served up for them.

As they were eating, Fernald told them he had made arrangements for four men to come from the Customs House and help in the capture of the band.

"That will give us five men, and with the element of surprise in our favor, we will have little trouble in capturing them," he said.

"How do you figure five?" broke in Dick.

"Why, myself, and the four men who are coming," he answered.

"Well, where do we come in?" demanded Phil, seconded by Garry.

"Oh, I had forgotten about the possibility of you're wanting to be there. I'm afraid that it is too dangerous," said Fernald gravely.

The protests of the three came almost in one voice, until Fernald, unable to keep a straight face any longer, broke out into a shout of laughter. The boys then saw that he had been indulging in a quiet bit of fun at their expense, and they were not to be cheated out of their share in the capture of the outfit.

After supper the boys pitched in and helped wash and wipe dishes, although Miss Ruth protested. Used as they were to camping, washing dishes was no new experience to them.

A pleasant evening was passed, and then the chums trooped off to bed, Fernald sharing the big room with them.

"Just think, while we are sleeping, LeBlanc and his outlaws will be coming across the border with their cargo of furs," said Dick, as they prepared for bed. "And we don't get any excitement now till the night after tomorrow. It will seem an age, the waiting."

They were up with the sun, and after breakfast Fernald left to loiter around the town, and see what could be seen, or hear any gossip. Of course by this time LeBlanc knew that Phil had been rescued, so Fernald judged that the safest thing for the boys to do was to keep either in the house or close to it, thus giving LeBlanc the idea that the trio had decided that discretion was the better part of valor, and had gotten out of such a dangerous locality.

"I'd like to have seen LeBlanc's face when he found out that Phil had given him the slip. I'll bet he was mad enough to chew nails," chuckled Garry.

The day did not prove half so long in passing as the boys expected that it would. Mr. Everett told them many a tale of the early days on the border, and other stories of smugglers along the coast line, where he first entered the Customs service.

There was a piano in the parlor, and the boys found that Ruth played in excellent manner, and found hearty enjoyment in singing while she played. Garry was greatly pleased to find that Mr. Everett played chess, and they enjoyed several games.

Fernald returned in the evening with the report that LeBlanc had not put in an appearance, but that Green had been much in evidence all through the afternoon, and wore an aspect of being greatly pleased.

"Tomorrow night he won't be quite so tickled about things as he appeared to be this afternoon," the agent remarked.

"Tomorrow night is a long way off, wish it was tomorrow night right now," half grumbled Phil.

"Patience, my boy, patience. You know all things come to those who wait," said Mr. Everett.

Mr. Everett had gained considerably in strength, and with the exception of his broken arm, was as well as ever, showing what a fine healthy constitution he possessed.

The second day seemed to be even longer in passing, for staying so much in the house began to pall on the boys, who craved excitement.

In the later afternoon, the four men from the Customs House came, arriving singly. They gathered in the big dining room, and there received instructions from Fernald, who had assumed the lead.

The instructions were simple. The boys were to lead them to the "lane," as they called it, and there they would deploy slightly and lay in wait for the quarry.

"I procured at the Customs House a star shell, such as was used during the war. When the men are over the line, and almost upon us, I will light it, and each one will pick a man and cover him. There will probably be seven of them, LeBlanc and Green, their two aids, the two Russians, and the man Anderson that you boys speak of. There are eight of us here, and we will be joined when we start out by the sheriff of this county and two deputies, who will arrive here after dark. That makes a force of eleven, enough to do the work."

"You mean there are twelve of us," broke in Everett. "I am going to be the twelfth man. Just because one arm is laid up doesn't mean that the other one cannot do double duty."

All protests were unavailing, and rather than deny him the pleasure of being one of the party, Fernald allowed that he could go, first demanding and getting a promise that if there should be a mix-up he would lose no time in getting to safety.

"We'll lay back a bit from the spot where they cross, because the arrest must be made on this side of the border, otherwise we would get in a jam with our neighbors to the north of us, and the arrest would not be valid, for they are not smugglers till they have crossed the line. One of your duties, boys, will be to keep your flashlamps going after the star shell has dimmed. That will last long enough to show them our force, and I anticipate no resistance."

Shortly after dark fell, the party was joined by the sheriff and his two deputies, and the little force, led by the three chums, made their way over the course taken the morning they set out in search of the point of crossing made by the smugglers.

Walking in Indian file, with no conversation other than an occasional direction or order given in a low tone of voice, they reached the border line. The boys felt a thrill of excitement at the thought of the part they were playing on this adventurous night. Soon they reached the point where Garry had watched, and from then on, Dick was the sole guide. Flashing his lamp only often enough to find the trail marks he had left, he led the way unerringly to the point where he had seen them cross.

There was no light save the feeble bit given by the stars, for it was in the dark of the moon.

"Now," whispered Dick to Fernald, "it was at this point that they crossed the border."

"All right, now men, follow me."

Fernald led the way back about twenty feet, having received the assurance of Everett, who was thoroughly familiar with that part of the country, that they were on the American side, and ordered the men to lay down, keeping their rifles and revolvers constantly at hand.

"No man is to make a move till I explode the star shell, then each one here pick a man. If orders are implicitly obeyed, there will be no trouble and no bloodshed."

"Beg pardon, sir," said Garry. "If we are laying down and you explode the shell, we'll be at a disadvantage, losing precious seconds in springing to our feet. I suggest you and I stay close together, and a few seconds before you are going to explode the shell, give me two taps on the shoulder. Then I can give the cry of a hoot owl, and each man can jump to his feet to be ready when the shell lights up the surroundings."

"Fine. Every man here know the cry of an owl?"

All did, so Fernald gave the order to lie down. The long, long minutes dragged into an hour, and the hour into a second. The boys were so restless that it was hard to lie quiet and still, but they forced themselves to.

It was almost midnight, but it seemed like a week to the boys, when the cracking of twigs and the crunch of feet warned of the approach of men. It proved to be the party, for they heard a low growling imprecation from Green as he stumbled over some object. Garry nudged Fernald, and immediately felt two sharp taps on his shoulder. At once he imitated the plaintive hoo-o-o- hoo-o-o- of an owl.

The men sprang to their feet. Fernald pressed the detonator of the star shell, tossing it into the air as he did so. It fell to the ground and shed its light, making it seem as bright and glaring as it would be in the noonday sun.

The attacked party halted as though turned to stone for a moment, so great was their surprise. Then Green let out a mighty cry.

They had no chance, for the businesslike rifles and revolvers of a dozen men were pointed straight at them. The two Russians were unarmed, and consequently unable to do anything had they wished. Every man gave up except one.

That was the half-breed, LeBlanc. With a cry of rage he fired his rifle into the midst of the men, fortunately hitting no one, and then turning, ran fleet as a deer back across the border. One of the deputies raised his rifle to shoot, but was speedily checked by Fernald.

"Shoot above his head to try and stop him, but don't hit him. He's on the other side of the border now!"

Then ordering the men to extend their hands, the Customs agents soon had them securely handcuffed.

Just at that moment an appalling thought came to Garry.

"Oh, Mr. Fernald. Suppose LeBlanc had the jewels!"

Truly the thought was a chilling one, but Fernald, always a man of action, made no reply, but sprang to the side of one of the Russians and searched him hastily but carefully. His search revealed nothing. Then he turned to the second, and in a minute uttered a jubilant shout.

"This fellow has a chamois money belt on, and unless I'm greatly mistaken, that's where the jewels are."

Making the Russian strip off his shirt, he unhooked the money belt, and while Garry held his light, examined the pockets.

Each one was crowded with magnificent gems that flashed under the rays of the flashlamp!

CHAPTER XX.

THE MAP AGAIN.

The men were marched away to the village, where they were incarcerated in the village lockup. In order that there would not be the slightest chance of their escaping, or being rescued by friends, who might in some way learn of their capture, Fernald ordered the Customs agents and the sheriff and his deputies to stand guard the rest of the night, keeping the prisoners constantly under surveillance.

Himself taking charge of the precious belt, he led the way to the Everett house. Here they found that Ruth had not retired, but had stayed up, nervously awaiting their return.

Carefully drawing the shades of the windows, Fernald emptied the pockets of the belt out onto the tablecloth.

For moments all stood spellbound at the beauty and magnificence of the gems.

Then Fernald, almost with awe in his voice, said:

"Why, there's a king's ransom here!"

After the party had examined the gems, and commented again and again on their beauty, it occurred to Ruth to ask what would be the disposal of the jewels.

"I imagine that in this case, since they are recovered after a theft, that an effort will be made to get in touch with the rightful owner. In the case of ordinary smuggled jewels, they would be seized by the United States. This, however, is a slightly different case. It is up to the department at Washington, where I shall go immediately to turn this fortune over to the proper persons. I confess, the quicker they get out of my care, the better I shall like it. They are too fabulously valuable to allow me to keep cool while in possession of them. Every minute I shall feel that someone is trying to get them. I'm off to Washington as soon as day comes, and I can get a train," concluded Fernald.

"And now, before we trot off to bed, what are your plans, boys? Will you return to Augusta to get your old station back again, or what?" asked the Customs man.

"Why, to tell you the truth, I should like a chance to stay here for two or three days and get a little hunting and fishing. We didn't have much chance for that while we were on this mission. I guess perhaps we could wire the Chief Ranger and ask for a little furlough. Also, we must wire the Customs Chief that we have done our work. I think probably the boys feel the same way that I do," said Garry.

"Well, if that is what you would like, it is very simple, and is a modest request. Leave that all to me. I'll stop off at Augusta and fix it for you. By the way, now that everything is all over, I may as well tell you that I am in complete charge of all Customs agents and houses for the entire northeastern part of the United States, so I guess I have influence enough to get your furlough fixed up for you," said Fernald, to the surprise of the boys.

Mr. Everett, however, proclaimed at once:

"I knew that all the time."

"Yes, I fancy you did," he said with a smile. "Now, I'm for a few minutes' sleep before morning train time."

"Yes, I guess we can all use a little," said Everett.

All trooped off to bed, having been told by Everett first that they could sleep until nine, as there was no train out that Fernald could take until ten o'clock, and he would have time for breakfast before starting back for Washington.

Rising time came all too soon, and the boys walked to the station to see Fernald off. Then they went back to the Everett house to get their rifles, and bid them goodbye, for they wanted to be off for their lean-to in the woods, there to plan out how to spend the week furlough they were depending on Fernald to secure for them.

They found the lean-to as they had left it, and their knapsacks and groceries were retrieved from their caches in the trees, as safe and sound as they were when they were put there some days before.

"I wonder if we are safe from LeBlanc?" asked Garry.

"I should say yes to that question, Garry," answered Phil. "He has been beaten at every turn. His friends are on their way to jail in Bangor, to be held for hearing before the United States Commissioner there, and he knows that the Customs service men will be relentless in their watch for him now that he has broken the law of the country. Besides, we shall soon be away from here, for I suggest we hike out soon for Lake Umculos, which is about thirty miles from here, and get some good fishing. The lake trout ought to be biting fine just about now, and we could get in some good swimming too, and that would please old heavyweight Dick."

Dick, as some of our readers know, was like a fish in the water, as most fat people are.

As they prepared lunch over the campfire, Phil broke out with:

"Do you know, fellows, in the stress and excitement of the past few days, we have never given a thought to the adventure of the lumberjack's boarding house, and the map that was bequeathed me by the old man just before he died? I wonder if there isn't some way we can dope out what the rest of it was. And while I'm asking questions, here are two more. What became of the tramps, and who was it that so carefully fixed up the shack at the deserted logging camp?"

"That's quite a bundle of questions, Phil," said Garry with a laugh. "To try and answer the first one, I am afraid that it is impossible. All we have to go on is that you start somewhere from the mouth of some small ravine. There is no telling how many small ravines there are in the State of Maine. Guess that is just a mysterious page in our book of adventures. As for the tramps, the fact that they were in this part of the country at all, points to just one theory, and that is, that having jumped bail, they are making tracks for the boundary line, thus getting themselves out of the country, so there will be less danger, if any, of their being captured and brought to trial. As for the last question, that too is a mystery, but there is one thing we can do, if you want to postpone your trip to the lake for two or three days, that is, solve the mystery. What's the vote?"

"I'm for solving a mystery any day in preference to fishing. We can fish almost anytime, and the lakes will keep, but we don't have a nice mystery served up on a silver platter everyday," announced Dick.

"That's my vote," agreed Phil.

"Then the question seems to be carried. The chair will now entertain a motion for the mode of procedure," announced Garry in a parliamentary tone.

The boys reflected for a moment or two, and then a suggestion was offered by Phil.

"Seems to me that the only way to do anything is to keep watch there for a while. We could take turns at it, while the other two took hikes or did a little hunting. We could take it in half day shifts, for it isn't very far from here."

"That seems the only feasible thing to do, but how could we keep watch without the person or persons who inhabit that place discovering our presence?" asked the practical Garry.

"There's one way out of that difficulty," offered Dick, "and that is to effect an entrance to the big bunkhouse, and rig up some sort of a peephole, and keep watch of the place in that manner. It is unlikely that place would ever be entered by those who are using the shack. Then here's another thing. You could rig your wireless here, and use one of the sending sets in the bunkhouse, so that the lookout could summon help if necessary."

"The bunkhouse idea is great, really it's the only feasible way. But the wireless 'phone is not such a good idea. It would entail staying right here all the time waiting for a possible message, and would be too irksome, besides losing all chance of hunting or fishing. I for one am anxious to try that trout brook old Dud told us of. Besides, there should be no especial danger, if there was I'd advise against having anything to do with it. Shall we draw lots for the first whack at watching?"

This was agreeable to all, and Garry drew watch number one, which they decided was to begin in the morning. All three would go to the bunkhouse, effect an entrance, and plan a way of speedy exit in case of need.

After lunch they overhauled their fishing tackle, and made for the brook, determined to catch a good mess of trout for their supper that night. Starting for the spring, they followed the course of the brook, until they reached a place where it was considerably wider and deeper.

Under the natural culvert, formed by the trunk fallen across, they cast their lines, using flies from their hook. Not having rods with them on this trip, they were forced to use slender saplings, but they were after food and not sport, so they did not mind pursuing the amateur way of flipping the fish on shore without playing him in the fashion dear to the hearts of anglers.

"If we go to the lake, we'll make up for this, for we can procure rods there, and have a real battle with some of those fine big lake trout," promised Garry.

"There isn't much sport to this, it is true," remarked Phil, as he flipped a fine specimen weighing at least three-quarters of a pound to the shore, "but they're going to be mighty fine eating just the same."

The fish were biting unusually well, and in less than no time they had a fine mess sufficient for supper. Returning to the lean-to, they cleaned the fish, and then spent the rest of the afternoon lounging about, for they had lost much sleep in the past two or three days, and no one was feeling particularly spry.

They had the fried fish, garnished with bacon, and hot biscuits and jam for supper, with of course the coffee that always goes with an out-of-door meal.

As soon as it was dark, they rolled in their blankets, and with their feet to the fire, were soon deep in sleep.

They were up with the dawn, and after breakfast headed towards the deserted logging camp. They approached carefully, and when within sight of it, waited and reconnoitered.

"Guess no one is at home or there would be a sign of smoke from the chimney, unless whoever is living there is eating raw food. Let's take a look at the spring," said Garry.

At the spring they found no sign of anyone having been there lately. This was easily seen, for the ground was soft about the bubbling spring, and would have retained a fresh print.

"All right then, now for the bunkhouse," ordered Garry.

They entered by prying loose one of the shutters and hopped inside. The interior gave no sign of having been used for years, as the dust was thick everywhere, and nothing could be found that looked as though it had been touched in some time.

In an old cupboard they found a box of nails of all sizes, and this gave Garry an idea. Cutting his bandanna handkerchiefs in strips, he doubled them up, until he had oblong pieces about two inches in width and four in length. Then he removed the shutter entirely, and fastened the cloth hinges he had made to it. While the others held the shutter in place again, he fastened the other ends of the crude hinges to the top of the window casing. A piece of string from his pocket was utilized to hold it tight against the bottom of the sill.

"You see, this string holds the shutter in place, and from the outside no one would ever suspect that it had been touched. You see I've used a window that is not in view of the shack. Now should it become necessary for any reason to leave this place in a hurry, a sharp push will break the strings that holds the shutter in at the bottom, and pushing out the shutter, it's only a matter of seconds in getting out. Then you can use your legs in getting clear of the vicinity," explained Garry.

At the opposite end of the shack, in a shutter, was pierced a peephole that commanded a view of the door of the shack that the boys believed was the one used by the occupant or occupants of the building.

"There, everything is set. You chaps hike, and then Dick is to return at noon to relieve me, leaving Phil the first watch tomorrow morning," ordered Garry.

Garry's watch was unavailing, for when Dick came at noon he had nothing to report. It was arranged that no one should come for Dick, but that he should be back as soon after dusk set in as possible. In order to be sure of Dick's safety, it was agreed that if he were not back by eight o'clock the others should come and see what was up, or if anything was the trouble.

Dick turned up at the lean-to just as dark set in, and reported that there was nothing stirring.

The boys were almost of the opinion that the whole business was a wild goose chase, but Phil was determined to take a hand at watching, and it was agreed that he should stand the morning watch, and be joined at noon by the others, who would finish the day together.

In case nothing developed they would put an end to the watching and start for Umculos Lake the following morning.

Phil started for his post the next morning. As he went, he said:

"I've a hunch something breaks this morning, hope my hunch comes true."

He had been gone not much more than an hour when he came tearing back, just catching the others as they were setting out on a short hike into a new and unexplored part of the woods.

"The mysterious occupant has come, and guess who it is!" he shouted.

"LeBlanc?" questioned Garry.

"The tramps?" hazarded Dick.

"Both wrong. It's the chap who was in the room with the old man in that house in Bangor. The one who got away with the missing portion of the map!"

CHAPTER XXI.

THE QUEST OF THE MINE.

"Well, talk about luck!" shouted Dick. "Let's dig back there as fast as we can, and rescue the missing portion of the map. He cannot have found the mine, for his part of the map was as useless to him as the part you have, Phil, was to us."

This seemed to be the best course to pursue, for the missing portion of the map was Phil's by every right, legally and morally, and they felt they had a right to pursue any tactics to get it back in their possession.

Without waiting to make any special plans, they secured their rifles and hatchets, but dispensed with their knapsacks, and left post haste for the old logging camp.

So fast was their hike that they were almost breathless when they arrived within sight of it.

Calling a halt, Garry bade them get their breath back, and then proposed a council to see what was to be done.

"I think it would be a good idea to try and pry off that window shutter. One of us can stand guard at the front door, the other at the rear, and the third can play with the window. In that way we can cover all retreat. There is a possibility of his being armed, of course, but that is a chance that we must take," suggested Phil.

"I think I know a better scheme than that," interrupted Garry. "What do you do when a coon takes refuge from the dogs in a tree?"

Both of his hearers were silent for a moment, and then Dick burst out:

"Why, you smoke him out of course!"

"Exactly. That is what I propose to do with this fellow."

They gathered a quantity of dry brush, and then proceeded to wet a portion of it in the spring.

"What are we going to do about letting it down the chimney? If we drop it all the way to the fireplace the chap can put it out, and if we use a piece of lariat, it will burn it off," said Phil.

"I thought of that, and have a solution for you. When Dick and I started for our hike, or rather were about to start when you came back with the news, we thought we might climb a tree or two, and so we put some wire in our pockets to use for a ring in climbing. That will work like a charm and drive him out in no time," answered Garry.

The wet and dry brush was rolled into a sort of a bundle, care being taken so that there was enough dry wood and twigs to catch fire properly. When these had caught fire, the wet brush would burn less easily, and cause a thick acrid smoke to be given off.

The bundle was then secured with a piece of the wire, while the other was attached to it by an end. At the other end of the free wire, a hook was bent, so that it could be hung over the edge of the chimney, allowing the smoking bundle to drop about two feet down the chimney.

"I'm counting on this chap thinking that the shack may be on fire, and will not investigate the chimney and try to pull the bundle down," said Garry, "so we must make no more noise than is absolutely necessary."

Cautiously they approached the house, and here Dick and Garry, being the heaviest, formed a sort of a human ladder and allowed Phil to mount to their shoulders. It was then easy for him to clamber noiselessly to the roof.

The bundle of brush was thrown up to him, and then they stripped their coats off and tossed these to him. The coats were to lay over the top of the chimney and keep the smoke from following its natural course upward.

In a few moments the bundle of brush was afire and in the chimney.

"Now we'll get action in a little while," opined Garry.

He was not mistaken, for in a minute they heard the sound of some one hurriedly groping at the fastenings of the back door. They raised their rifles and trained them on the door.

Phil had slipped down from the top of the roof and joined them, making a sizable force to greet the illegal owner of the piece of map they so much desired.

The door was thrown open and the man dashed out, to stare in a bewildered manner at the tree. Upon Garry's sharp order, he elevated his hands skyward and then asked what they wanted.

"We want a certain piece of paper that you got away with a few nights ago in an old boarding house on Canal street in Bangor," said Phil. "Out with it!"

A cunning look crept into the man's eyes, which Garry did not fail to detect.

"I threw it away right after I left the house, because I didn't know what it was all about or whether it was any good," he declared.

"I don't believe you," said Garry promptly. "Dick and Phil, you keep your guns trained on him. I'm going to slide through his pockets."

At these words, the man involuntarily looked down at his chest. Garry noted this glance, and immediately decided that the search would not have to go further than the two pockets in the woollen shirt the man was wearing.

The two boys closed in on him, with their rifles-pointing directly at his head, while Garry advanced to look through the shirt pockets. The man looked for a moment as though he were about to resist, but the sight of the two rifles made him use common sense.

The first pocket revealed nothing, but in the second was an old envelope, and in this was a piece of paper which at a glance was recognized as the missing portion of the map. With this in his hands, Garry backed away.

"Now," he said sharply, "this belongs to us. It was given by the dying man to our chum here. We are not going to give you in custody, for the coroner found that the man had not died by foul play. However, if we catch sight of you again, you will be seized and given to the authorities, and a charge of

133

theft of this paper from us will be lodged against you. Now dig out of here. You have three minutes before we shoot. Forward, march!"

"Can I get my blanket?" asked the man.

"Certainly, and anything else you have in the shack, only we'll go in with you while you get it," answered Garry.

Sullenly the man went in and got his blanket and what tinned food there was left, also a hand axe which he stuck in his belt. He had no weapon other than a wicked hunting knife, and this he was allowed to keep. Muttering threats under his breath, he left the shack, and started slowly up the trail to the town, stopping once or twice to look back and shake his fist meantime to see if the boys meant business. Finally Garry lifted his rifle and sent a shot whistling several feet over the man's head. Immediately he put on a burst of speed that didn't decrease until he was far out of sight.

"That's that. I think we have seen the last of him," said Garry.

As a matter of fact, this was the last they saw of him, for he never stopped until he reached the station, where he hid until he had a chance to steal a ride on the rods of a freight train.

Back at the lean-to, they pieced the map together again, and were able to find the second missing location. According to the remainder of the note, mark number two consisted of three great stumps, close together in triangular form. The directions were to dig between them, where the secret of the mine would be disclosed.

Garry fished out a map of the State, and found that the Shohela river ran not more than forty miles away. The town of Jennings was marked, and proved to be a small village, deserted almost in the summer, for the tourists had not penetrated to that section, but quite a center in the winter for lumberjacks coming and going to their work in the woods.

The river itself was used for the log drives in the spring. Somewhere above was the bend in the river, from where they could guide their steps until they found the secret mine. Just what kind of a mine it would prove to be, none of the boys had any idea. It would hardly be silver or gold, for there never had been one found in that State. They thought there was a chance of there being copper, as in Wisconsin there were great copper mines.

Figuring out their course, they decided to start that afternoon, and by easy marching, arrive at Jennings late the following day.

They repacked their knapsacks, using part of the food they had stored in the tree cache, and then left the remainder of it in the lean-to with a note addressed to old Dud, saying he could have it, and bidding him goodbye for the time being.

They intended to come back after they had found or failed to find the lost mine and say goodbye to the Everetts.

After a march of about five hours, they camped under the trees for the night, and were soon eating a supper cooked over the open campfire. For safety's sake they kept sentry duty up through the night, not fearing anyone in particular, but with the idea that an ounce of prevention was worth a pound of cure.

After breakfast they took up the march again, stopping an hour for lunch, and then resuming the journey, reached Jennings just at sunset.

"Let's dodge the town altogether for the present, and go around it, and find a spot where we can camp for the night. Then in the morning we can follow the river up its course till we come to the bend mentioned in the note on the back of the map," suggested Dick.

This suggestion met with the approval of the others, and so they circled Jennings, and found a desirable place to sleep and eat.

Sun-up found them awake, and after a hasty breakfast, so anxious were they to find the mine, they made for the river bank, without losing time.

Up the river they went, getting more and more excited with each step. A walk of less than an hour brought them to what was unmistakably the bend in the river that was the first mark noted in the note. Here, using the sun as a guide, they proceeded east for the necessary two miles. True enough, here was a ravine, small enough, but still a ravine. The region was only sparsely wooded, and the boys knew enough about geology, which they studied the preceding winter at school, to know that the formation of the land in that section was quite rocky, there being evidence of much granite.

"You don't suppose the old chap that fixed that note was mixed in his terms through ignorance, and meant that there was a good granite quarry there, do you?" asked Dick dubiously.

"Never can tell," answered Garry. "Only thing to do is follow directions and see what happens."

Following directions, they paced about a mile and a half, keeping a sharp lookout for the triangle of stumps. To make sure they would not miss it, they deployed and marched about twenty paces distant from each other. Phil was the one to spy the landmark. His shouts brought the others running to him.

"Let's dig, and dig quick," pleaded Phil. "I want to see if we've found a fortune, or are only the victims of a practical joke, or gigantic hoax."

The others were as curious as he, and using their axes, as a sort of combined pick and shovel, dug away at the ground surrounded by the stumps. In a few minutes, Phil's axe struck something hard, and abandoning his axe, he scratched the earth away with his fingers. The hard something was a tin can, evidently, about which had been wound several feet of tape such as is used to repair bicycle punctures and such. Fishing his knife from hispocket, Phil proceeded to cut away the taping, while the others, with bated breath, awaited the result of the find. It took some minutes to scrape and cut away the hardened tape, but at last it was accomplished.

Tearing the cover from the can, they found an old envelope, which was soon opened, disclosing a letter, written in the same cramped hand as was the note whose directions had guided them there. It said:

"One hundred paces due east from here is a sharp ridge of granite, that projects above ground for nearly thirty feet. After the granite enters the ground, there the treasure begins. I know it is there, for I have been a miner all my life, and know geology as well as though I had gotten it out of books. The granite ridge is rich in quartz and in tourmalines. I got some out and had them cut and polished, and they are the finest ever found in Maine. This secrecy is necessary, due to the fact that a partner who went back on me has tried to wrest the secret from me, also the fact that I must wait until I can buy the land the ridge is on from its owners."

The three boys stared at each other.

"Tourmalines," said Garry. "Why, those are the semi-precious stones known as the State of Maine gem. They are delicate pink and green, and whencut make beautiful stones for jewelry. Don't you chaps recollect the ring my mother wears? Well, that is a pink tourmaline. As far as I know, they are found in only three other places in the State. If there is any quantity of them, there is a neat sum of money to be made by mining them. Let's go and look at the ridge and see if we can see anything, although I doubt it, since they are under ground and we have nothing to dig properly with, neither have we geologists' hammers or blasting powder to shelve off parts of the ledge. Also, we don't own this land, and would be liable under the law as trespassers."

They paced their way to where the ridge was, and looked at it carefully. It gave evidence of having been blasted two or three times, but they could see nothing that looked like the matrices of the tourmaline gems.

"Well, we know all about it, and can find it again, so I move we destroy all notes about it, and telegraph Dad to see if he can find out who owns this. He will know, because you see at no little distance from here begins timberland, and he knows who owns most of the big tracts. Phil, you are in luck."

"Why me?" asked Phil in surprise.

"Because the old fellow made you his legatee by his spoken last will and testament. All that remains is for you to buy about an acre of this ground for your operations, and get busy mining," answered Garry.

"Not by a long shot. We've shared our dangers together. Twice you boys have rescued me from death, and this mine will remain a secret for someone else to find out about unless you fellows go in on a share and share alike basis. I mean that, absolutely flat, and won't listen to any discussion or debate about it," declared Phil in resolute tones.

Both Dick and Garry attempted to argue with him, but he was firm and at last they agreed. At first it was decided to call it the Ranger Mine, and then Phil, with a nudge at Dick, proposed that they call it the Ruth Mine, and give her the first gem taken out, as a testimonial for the help she had given them in their quest for the smugglers. Garry reddened like a beet, and thought he was being joshed, but seeing Phil was serious, they voted it to be so.

"Now back to Jennings and the telegraph office, and start the ball rolling for the purchase of some of that land, and then maybe we win a fortune, and again perhaps we don't, but it's worth a chance," said Garry.

CHAPTER XXII.

CONCLUSION.

They found that they could send a telegram from the railroad depot, and so Garry addressed the following query to his father:

"Can you find out immediately who owns land about five miles west of Jennings, just at edge of what appears to be big lumber tract. If not, can you refer us to someone in Jennings who knows? Important, rush answer.

GARRY."

"Now all we can do is wait for the answer. In the meantime, let's look around the town a bit," said Garry.

This they did, but found little to see. They did not care to inquire about the ownership of land from anyone in the town, as it would mean dodging the questions of the curious natives of the little village.

Several trips were made to the station, and finally they got an answer. It said:

"I do. Why?

FATHER."

The boys did a war dance on the platform, giving the station agent good cause to think they were a little bit touched in the head.

Garry immediately sent the following telegram:

"Have made important discovery. Do not under any circumstances, please, sell the land till you get letter from us, which leaves today.

"GARRY."

Borrowing Dick's ever ready notebook, and tearing out several of the pages, Garry wrote a long note telling of the discovery and asking that they be allowed to buy an acre of the land, since they had discovered the mine, or if they couldn't buy an acre for any reason, that they be allowed to purchase the mineral rights, and lease enough land for operations. He told his father to address him at Hobart, care of John Everett.

The letter was dispatched special delivery, and then Garry said:

"It will take this letter at least two days to reach Dad, and by that time we will be back in Hobart. Then it will take two days for the letter to get back, perhaps three, and we can have a bit of a vacation in that time, and get a better look at Hobart and see something of the town."

"And see something of the pretty little granddaughter too," said Phil in a low tone to Dick.

"I wish you fellows would stop ragging me about that. I think she's nice and pretty and all that, but why try and make a romance? Why, we're nothing but boys yet, plenty of time to think of love and romance after school and college," protested Garry, blushing.

"Course you're only a boy, but that doesn't stop you greatly admiring the young lady, and of course Phil and I are only boys, but that doesn't mean that we don't have eyes and brains in our head and don't see through you like a piece of glass," and the fat boy laughed till his sides shook, at the blushing face of his good chum.

"Well, that's enough of that. Let's take a good chunk out of the journey back to Hobart today, and get there by mid-afternoon tomorrow. Let's fill our canteens and get going," ordered the leader.

The return trip was made without any unusual event, and they repaired at once to the Everett home, where Ruth and her grandfather were told of the discovery, under the pledge of secrecy.

The young lady was evidently more than pleased about the mine being named for her. Mr. Everett was as right as a trivet again, barring the fact that his arm was of course still in bandages and splints.

For the next two days they hiked about the country, with Mr. Everett as guide, of course accompanied by Ruth, and heard many tales of that section in the early days.

Finally the long-looked-for letter came, and as it bears on the succeeding adventures of the boys, it will be given:

"DEAR GARRY:

"As I told you in the telegram, I own that land. I have a wide strip there for a right of way for that timber tract to the river. Of course you boys may have it, but I suggest that you lease it and the mineral rights. I will sell you the lease for one dollar, just to make it legal, and the mineral rights I freely give you three boys as a present in pay for something that you are going to do for me very shortly. It will necessitate getting a leave of absence from the Ranger Service, but I can arrange that. Meet me in Bangor, as soon as possible, at the Bangor House.

"I will be waiting your arrival. I cannot tell you much about it now, except that you may have a chance to play a part in a big timber war. All this will be explained to you when I see you. Congratulations from all of us in your success in the smuggler capture. The Chief has written all about it to me.

As ever,

"DAD."

"Hurrah! Here's a chance for new adventures. We'll take the next train and be on our way. Boys, this is some summer. Fires and captures and smugglers and a treasure mine discovered, and now a timber war. All aboard," shouted Dick.

Bidding the Everetts goodbye, and promising to keep in constant touch with them, they went to the station, where, luckily, a train was soon due.

Of the stirring adventures of the boys in the great timber country, and how they circumvented a group of timber thieves who were bent on ruining Mr. Boone, and more about LeBlanc, will be told in the next book, Volume Four of the Ranger Boys, entitled, "THE RANGER BOYS OUTWIT THE TIMBER THIEVES."

THE END

Milton Keynes UK
Ingram Content Group UK Ltd.
UKHW010625250923
429338UK00004B/340